THIS LOVE OF MINE
Published by *The Bitter End Publishing*

Copyright © 2017 by Gina Danna
978-0-9896644-8-6

Printed in the USA.

Cover Design and Interior Format

THIS *Love* *of* MINE

Gina DANNA

To the
BITTER END
PUBLISHING

To the one who understands and supports this author and her wandering muse, whether its Ancient Rome, the Regency, Victorian England or the American Civil War. Thank you!

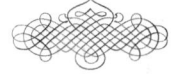

England 1810

JAMES HADDINGTON III, EARL OF Windhaven, basked in the sunlight that poured through the church's windows, a light that blazed a trail from the alter where he stood down the aisle to the young lady walking towards him. He couldn't help but smile at the vision before him. Not many bachelors welcomed the loss of their freedom, mostly due to marriages contrived of family status and advancement via marital ties, but for him, he'd found the perfect match. This marriage was based on love and, for that, he relished in the morning wedding ritual, dreaming of celebrating with his lovely bride as soon as he could steal her away from the guests at their wedding breakfast.

For he was in love with the lady who glided ever closer to him. Eleanor Whitmore stole his breath away. She was beauty and poise wrapped into one delectable package. Even now she was breathtaking, dressed in a pink and cream fashionable high-waist gown, lace lining her décolleté. Her spun sable hair was piled on her head in a mound of curls with a couple of strands coiling down her neckline, as if whispering to him to touch them. Her sapphire blue eyes danced and she had a faint smile on her rosy lips. A rush of heat spiraled down his spine to a fire in his loins, tightening his insides.

He had met her during last Season, a daughter of a viscount from some God-forsaken county in the north. Eleanor had a smile that would make any man melt and gaining her made many pledge to do whatever she wanted. They had all bowed to her but she gave her all to him, the Earl of Windhaven, and he to her. It was a match made in heaven and one he refused to give up, despite the higher ranking gentlemen pushing for her hand and a father that wanted wealth to insure his family for years to come. Not that James didn't have money, nor did he hold a title lower than her father's expectations. Much to the contrary. But the old man shot for higher rank, irritating James.

Eleanor, though, had her own motivation—love.

James spun her on the dance floor, his heart beating hard and fast to the sound of her laugh and the sparkle in her blue eyes. The petite waif captured his heart at their introduction and the touch of her gloved hand on his drove the nail home. He asked for her hand in marriage by the end of the dance and happily he recalled her response of yes, the unofficial acceptance followed by her father's approval. Within a month, before the end of the Season, their whirlwind romance led to a wedding on the most glorious sunny day in May…

He relished every breath he took with her by his side. Despite that, a quiet fear that this was only a dream haunted his thoughts. That he'd wake to find her not there and never had been. The fear hit at times so hard that he could not breath and he closed his eyes tightly, fighting that nightmare away. No, Eleanor was here, walking down the aisle to become his wife.

Memories of two mornings ago seeped into his thoughts in the final seconds before she stood next to him. When they had had the evening to themselves, the banns fully read and their wedding nothing more than a showpiece for the *ton*, since all would consider them bonded.

A simple kiss became deeper. To touch her finally brought home how slender and delicate she was but he soon discovered her need for him equaled his for her. He tried to take it slow, to not hurt her, but she gave him little hope of gentle seduction.

Now she was at his side. Her father placed her hand in his and she squeezed. He gave her a lopsided grin, a thank you, for returning him to the ceremony. It was a long, drawn out affair as the priest droned on about the sanctity of marriage and the prodigy it would produce, as if they were cattle, he thought snidely, all in the name of the Lord. He only halfway heard the churchman, too involved in touching her again, even with both of them wearing gloves.

Vows stated, they were blessed and off to a breakfast of cheer and well-wishes from their guests. He could not leave fast enough. Once he saw the opportunity, he scooped her away.

Finally back at the Windhaven estate, alone with his bride, he took her to the bedroom. No words were heard but their bodies spoke a million. Into late in the afternoon, his soul sang. Eleanor was here, her deep honey-brown mussed curls on his shoulder and she was cradled next to him, her sigh rustled the hairs on his chest, sending a shiver down his spine. By night, exhaustion overwhelmed them. He didn't sleep much but her soft, steady breath assured him she did. His beautiful Eleanor…

Her arm across his chest repositioned itself ever slightly, cuddling her body up close to his side. Dainty fingertips pressed against his breast before resting. It made his blood race with excitement. Oh, she had him and knew he'd never deny her. It was a game, part of the seduction, to find that point of no return. Their destroyed bedchamber a testimony to that with clothes everywhere, the main blanket thrown aside, using only a bed sheet and their body heat to warm them through the night.

Finally, her lips touched his upper arm, and as they pressed against his flesh, flames ignited inside him. It took every ounce of energy not to quiver.

She moved closer. Her breasts, delicate and delicious mounds of womanly flesh, pushed against him. When she touched him, her nipples were hard and the air began to fill with the scent of her. Her thighs were wrapped around his hips and the heat of her feminine lips, wet with need, dripped on him.

"Its chilly in here." She shivered against him.

Liar. It was the end of May, the heat of summer was slowly turning up as the morning took hold but he said nothing.

He chuckled. "No, my love. You feel very warm to the touch."

She kissed his arm then moved to his chest. "Then heat my insides. Make love to me, my darling James…"

Her words unraveled his resolve to hold back and let her body mend from all the play earlier. With a growl, he turned slightly, grabbed her hips and rolled, placing her on top of him, his harden cock balanced between the apex of her thighs but not inside her. It was total torture to have her spread over him, the warmth of her wet heat coating his stiffened, throbbing member.

"James, please."

He gazed at her face, thrilled at her straddling him, her eyes clouded with desire, her nipples pearled and dark pink with her long, blonde hair cascading over her shoulders. It took him only a second to lift her hips, allowing his hardened cock to pivot to the right spot. He slowly lowered her, impaling her slick passage till he filled her.

They kept their eyes locked, even as the pace quickened. Her breasts bobbed and he reached for one, pinching the nubbed rosette with each twist, issuing little groans from her lips. Slowly he rose to suckle from her—only a second before her hips rocked back.

As her core tightened, his own assent to climax escalated, the very notion of shooting his seed into her womb drove him further till he couldn't take it any longer and he grabbed her hips, flipping their position with him on top, still buried inside. With a husky moan, she grinned and locked her legs around his hips as he ground into her. She mewled a protest when he pulled back, his tip barely inside and that drove him over the edge. He sank into her and, before he let himself go, she quivered, shattering around him. He quickly joined her, his seed streaming into her body as he collapsed on top of her.

Still inside, he panted, trying to regain composure with her legs still around his hips.

"I love you, James." She kissed his lips lightly.

He smiled at his queen. "I love you, Eleanor. Now and forever." He returned her kiss more thoroughly. As he pulled away, she smiled with a sigh.

His life was complete.

Chapter One

HER BROWS BUNCHED IN A frown as she tilted her head, assessing herself in the looking glass. When she realized what she was doing, she snorted at the ugly reflection and straightened, wiping the look from her face. She could hear her mother reminding her that she'd cause age lines by frowning so much. And the voice inside her head made her smile. Her dear mama had parted this life two years ago, making a void in her heart she didn't think would mend until she met James…

She adjusted the ivory bonnet and retied the bow, deciding it was right and smart looking. Her cream pelisse, trimmed in blue, shifted on her shoulders and she turned for an overall view of how it appeared with her new ivory and blue striped silk gown, trimmed in lace and ribbons. But even a small turn made her wince as an ache from her core out to her hips reminded her how her new husband pleasured her repeatedly last night. A small smile spread to her lips as the memories flooded her, stoking the fire in her lower abdomen to simmer with desire, even weeks after they had wed. She closed her eyes simply to enjoy the marks left by his touch…

"Be careful, darling. I can still taste you," a deep, husky masculine voice whispered into her ear. "I may take you back to bed."

She giggled. "As I recall, my lord, you claimed you had appointments to keep, as do I."

With a distant eye, Eleanor peered at their reflection in the mirror and saw a portrait of a loving couple, standing together, his arms wrapped around her waist. He was a handsome man, one that caused a flutter to start in her stomach, one that grew to a heated frenzy. Now, her need rekindled, despite the soreness of their repeated lovemaking. Leaning back against his rock hard chest, the heat of him permeated the silk dress, right through her stays and down to her very bones. He towered above her. His dark brown hair was short considering the style most of his peers wore. With piercing blue eyes that danced in the flames of passion when they were in bed, James made her happy. Tall, broad-shouldered, tapered waist, he was a man made of hours in the saddle. He loved to take his horse on wild steeplechases, running the hills, and fencing. Still intertwined in his arms, she turned simply so she could trace the contours of his chest, fascinated by the lines wrought from the physical work.

The tendons in his arms flexed and she melted a bit more against him. Yes, she loved him with her whole heart and that alone made her feel secure. She had started to believe that despite all the dances and soirees of the Season and all the men who attended, looking for a wife, that she'd never find love. A husband, yes, but never the delirious joy this man had set her on.

James smirked. "Continue that, my love, and no one will see us." He kissed her neck, just below her ear.

A heavy sigh escaped her lips. "Will it always be like

this?"

He nuzzled behind her ear. "I pray it will be." He pulled back and turned her to face him. "You best be on your way as I expect Wilkinson and Clearwater here shortly. Now," he gave her a hard look. "Without me by your side, I wish you'd take something to defend yourself with, in case the need arises."

She didn't like the stern look on his face. "Darling, there is nothing to fear. I will have Matty with me. And you do have the driver and coachman with their firearms, which, I will say, make me a bit unnerved. No one else drives with that. The French are not here. Not in London nor on the city's outskirts. I will be fine."

James' gaze narrowed. "I will have my wife protected at all costs."

"I'm only going to Bond Str—"

"Precisely." He took her hands. "There are bandits out there, looking for unsuspecting prey. We are not in the heart of the city. Being just within driving distance is all these villains need, for they will look for a liveried coach bearing riches—"

"No one would touch the Earl of Windhaven's carriage. Your reputation precedes you." She smiled, tapping the tip of his nose with her finger. But the look of worry didn't ease in his gaze. Instead, his fingertip rolled gently above her décolleté beneath her pelisse, then dipped between her breasts to the top of her stays. With a slight twist of his fingers, he pried her busk free, pulling it out slowly.

"James," she murmured. It was an intimate move that sent heat spiraling down her spine before it dawned on her his expression hadn't changed. He didn't remove the piece entirely.

"Promise me, if set upon, you will not hesitate to use this."

She frowned. "Darling, it is—"

"A weapon, if needed. Promise me." He stood before her, hand still on the raised busk, the tone of his voice tense.

"Of course." She pushed his hand down, reasserting the make-shift knife back into place. She smiled. That combined with her promise seemed to break through his fierce gaze. It gave her the moment she needed to leave, if she was to keep her appointment. With a quick kiss to his lips, Eleanor grabbed her gloves and reticule and headed out the door, before he had another chance to stop her. Now, if she could only get her heated body to cool…

∞

JAMES SHUT HIS EYES, THROWING the pen in his hand to the desktop, and fell back into the padded chair. He was tense as a turned violin string. The lumbering clouds outside his library window had multiplied, darkening a sunny afternoon. The air had become thick. Rain. He could smell it in the wind. It was not a good time to be traveling. Storms could frighten even the most experience equine and roads could turn into muck and mire.

His Eleanor was out in this mess.

And any highwayman who rode the trails, looking for easy—and rich—prey.

He ran his fingers through his dark brown strands, trying to calm his nerves that even now had the hair on the back of his neck bristling. A crack of thunder had him on his feet, fear for her spread like wildfire through him.

He should not have let her go. Eleanor….

A single knock at the door, followed by his butler Benjamin opening it caught his attention.

"My lord, the Viscount of Clearwater requests to see

you."

The door behind the balding elderly servant swung wide open and Albert Clearwater, Viscount of Clearwater, busted into the room.

"No need for formalities, old chap!" He didn't slow till he got to James's desk, a broad grin on his lips and his eyes wide with excitement. "Not going to offer you friend a drink, James?"

James frowned and started to say something when another stag joined the herd.

"Perhaps, old man, after he offers one to his better friend," the newcomer challenged. George Wilkinson, the Marquis of Stonebriar. Wilkinson slapped Clearwater on the back and both broke into laughter, dragging the reluctant James to join them.

Biting back his chuckle as the two lords began their ceaseless banter on who was the better man, James pulled three glasses out of the sideboard and poured.

"I dare say, James, what has you so damn quiet, huh? That parcel you stole from us wearing you out? Not the young buck you claim to be?" Wilkinson took the glass and downed a gulp before James even heard the last word.

"Stonebriar, be kind." Clearwater took a glass. "Has years of service to Lady Stonebriar dulled the mind? Or is it that piece you cavort with? What was her name? Penelope?"

James took a sip, letting them distract him. He had to place his faith in God that Eleanor was fine and no doubt she was. The last thing she needed was him dogging her every step. But their eyes glued upon him had him breaking his silence.

"The Lady Windhaven is off for an afternoon with the ladies."

A heavy breeze, damp with the coming rain, came

through the window,

"In this muck and mire? Surely, she won't tarry long out of doors. A storm is coming." Clearwater sipped then he frowned. "On the road to London? Perhaps you have cause for concern. Highwaymen love the rain and what it can do to carriages."

Wilkerson shot Clearwater a look but James caught it. He knew it meant to shut him up, but the thoughts similar to that stated were already in his mind.

"I'm sure she is blessed and safely there. Your men are gallant enough to withstand any attack, of that I am assured." Wilkerson raised his glass and smiled. But it was a smile as vacant as the one James returned.

As thunder cracked the skies, James shut his eyes and prayed.

∞

THE ROAD WAS CHOPPY, JARRING the carriage periodically. The jolt virtually lifted Eleanor off the seat to drop her suddenly. At first, it startled her since she wasn't paying attention but fiddling with her bodice. James' attempt to make a point about her busk being used as a weapon had unsettled the stays. One was jabbing her side. The conveyance wheel hit a hole, lurching it for a split second, long enough to make her wince when her skin got pinched by her stays on the landing. So she braced herself as she fixed it. To make matters worse, the horses took off at a run, the driver yelling from his seat outside the enclosed carriage.

She frowned. There was no need to race to town. The skies had darkened but no thunder had set the team into a panic nor had lightning pierced the sky. Peering outside, she found it still dry and dust rose around them as the wheels increased frantically under the running equines.

Whipping wind raced through the opening, strong enough to rent her hat from her head despite the hatpin that she admitted she hadn't put in right.

"George! What in name of all that's holy are you doing?" She screamed out the window to the driver. But there was no response outside his urging the mounts to go faster. What were they running from? No one should be here, except...her thoughts faded until it hit her full side. High-waymen! Robbers! Turning in her seat, she took a peek out the small back window and found three horsemen barreling down on them.

Gunfire cracked the air, followed by George's whip snapping. Oh dear.....

One of the wheels hit another rut, sending the vehicle flying in the air. Eleanor wasn't prepared, still sitting with her back turned to view out the back window. When the gun fired, she slouched. The carriage bounced out of another hole and she was ejected from her perch, her head hitting the hard roof. It rattled her senses and pain shot through her skull.

The wagon skidded to a halt as the pounding hooves of the highwaymen's horses grew closer. She closed her eyes, trying to right herself. Spots danced before her when she tried to focus.

The side door flew open.

"Well, looky what we've git here." The male voice was cockney-accented. But her head hurt so much she couldn't pull away from him as he reached for her reticule. "Now be a good girl, er, lady, and hand it to me." He yanked it out of her hands and rummaged through the small bag.

She reached to take it back but the motion made her dizzy and she fell back on her seat. Outside the vehicle, she found George sprawled on the ground, blood smeared on his face, the sight of it made her want to gag and that only made her head throb more. Swallowing the bile in her throat, she braced herself, the growing desire to escape taking control. She pushed off the padded seat toward the door but the sudden motion set her off balance. Her hand caught the doorjamb right as a shot of pain enveloped her and then everything turned black.

Chapter Two

WHAT SEEMED AN ETERNITY OF darkness and quiet faded to the sound of voices, which were muddled. The ringing in her ears and the thudding in her temple made the situation only worse but if she stayed still, she could pick up a tone or two while trying to massage the pain in her head away with pressing on her temple. The talkers were masculine and argumentative. She really didn't care what they were ranting on about, but the sound became louder, which only increased her irritability because she wanted them to be quiet.

Her throat was dry, as if she'd swallowed sand, and her neck, shoulders, and head ached. She struggled to open her eyes, her lids way too heavy to lift, but she needed to find these two and shut their mouths before she did something outlandish.

With every ounce of energy she could muster, she rolled gently to her side. After a moment of relocating her balance, she tossed her legs over the side of the bed. She fought mentally for her bearings but discovered her wrists were lashed together. She tried to part them but caused more pain, this time racing up her arms to her shoulders. Next, she flexed her ankle and discovered her feet were free. Confused and hurting, she eased herself upright slowly.

What had happened?

She jogged her memory, searching through the murk clouding it. Images of the carriage, the sudden jolt of it racing before a storm, of men who shot poor George and reached for her… Then the scenes vanished.

As she sat, praying the hammer within would simply stop, she heard those voices again. Their heated discussion began to leak through the planked door and she concentrated, trying to pick up if they knew she was in here and why…

"You put us in a heap of trouble!"

"That ain't fair! You done told me to hit her, too!" The voice to this statement sounded childish, like a man with no spine.

"Joey, you truly are a dimwit! I tole you to git the girl, not to hit her! In the name of St. Michael & St. George…"

Ah, the man in charge, Eleanor decided. The one who apparently acted as if he could think. From the pain in her head, she assumed the other was a true thug.

"But Johnny, we do have her! Just like…."

Johnny snarled. "His lordness will not b' pleased."

A lord commanded that her carriage was to be attacked, her person abducted? Even with her throbbing head, she could count on no one in the nobility who would want to harm her…

"Well, she ain't dead. I knows." There was a rustling noise, like a hand hitting man's chest. "I done check on hcr a bit 'go and she breathin'."

Her eyes widened and instantly, she scanned herself as best she could. By looks, she hadn't been violated, outside being knocked unconscious, transported to here, wherever this is, and left tied. But a slight shift of balance on her seat reassured her that her lower core was left alone, for there was no ache.

"Then we bests be gittin ourselves cleaned," Johnnie blurted. "The hour is nearly here."

Their words rang home. Whoever hired them for this was en route and she'd be carried further away or hurt more, maybe killed. That thought sent a cold shiver down her spine. She tried to pull at the rope around her wrists to no avail. Frantically, she searched the room for a tool to cut them and in the dim light, found nothing outside the handful of wooden crates and barrels, along with the makeshift pallet she woke on. The building wasn't the best made. The room itself had no window but the sun's rays peeked through the wall's slat boards.

She had to think. She'd been captured and now held for some reason, supposedly by a member of the nobility, according to the dolt accomplices in the other room. A peep through the cracks in the wall showed her that Joey and Johnny were ill-kept, to the point of disgusting, with greasy hair. The one she decided must be the leader had a paunch stomach and Joey wore no shoes. The mere thoughts of their filthy hands touching her in any way made her want to retch. She swallowed hard to keep the bile down. The sound of losing her contents would alert them she no longer remained unconscious.

Instead, a sharp memory struck her. Of James fishing her busk out of her stays, murmuring something about a weapon. She bent her arms to try to retrieve the piece. It wasn't easy with her hands bound but she didn't have a choice. Her friends had certainly alerted her husband of her absence or James had heard of her abduction and had a party out looking for her, she was sure. She had to find a way out to be seen so he would find her. She bit her lip against the pinch that went deep as her fingernails parted the fabric and she touched the top of the busk. Every movement hurt but she managed to pry the piece free. Grasping the end between her teeth, she maneuvered the narrow end closer to her fingertips and the knot below. It wasn't a hard knot but one turned enough to make unraveling it hard without a tool. Now with one supplied, she worked frantically to unfasten it.

Johnnie and Joey still bickered, their words muted but they were involved enough and far from the door. As the roping unraveled, she flipped her wrists. Her hands prickled as blood raced into them, having turned numb from being tied so tight. Quickly, she caught the rope before it fell, deciding it might come in handy.

She eyed the opposite wall, away from the two highwaymen. The sun shined through this side more brightly, though she couldn't determine the time of day or if it was even the same day but there was faint noises of other people and the sound of water against ships and peers. Stepping closer to the wall, she discovered a lose piece of wood, like a splinter. She shoved the corset's busk back down her stay, wincing as it pinched the skin beneath. If she could slide the piece through an opening, maybe she could pry it loose. It took longer than she wanted but it worked and the rotten slat splintered and snapped. She cringed at the sound of it and knew now her captors might hear it. It was now a race to get free. Holding the prying wood piece tight to use as a weapon, deciding it was better than the rope. She inhaled to draw her body tight and slipped through the narrow opening.

The sunlight was so bright, it blinded her. She blinked, adjusting to it. The sound of splashing water came from the river below and the bellowing noises of dock workers and ships. It had to be the Thames River, bustling like it was though she'd never truly gotten this close as she recalled. She breathed deep, inhaling the scent of the river and her freedom.

A crash startled her. Behind her, the two captors peered through the open door to her cell. The stunned look on their faces as they saw her standing clear on the other side of the slatted wall gave her that brief moment to come to her senses and flee. As she darted down the wooden walkway, they yelled, splitting wood as they broke through the broken wall to chase her.

The dockworkers were busy, rarely glimpsing her way. She wanted to scream to them for help but found herself too winded, trying to run in a dress she had to scrunch up to clear her feet and the stays that confined her lungs. The two miscreants closed in. To reach the road meant running uphill, which would slow her down and allow them the advantage. Her other choice was to turn the opposite way and head downhill, toward the ships. It'd be easier and there were more men working down there, perhaps one would aid her. She turned and started down the wooden stairs to the docks.

Johnnie and Joey cursed loudly and started down the same path. Fear made her almost fly, until her toe hit a lump and she stumbled. Down the stairs she fell, banging her head and legs on each twist. She bit back the pain, tried to clear her thoughts after her head took a knock on the wooden railing. A couple of the dock workers looked up, a few started toward her but she couldn't decide if that was to help her or the two chasing her. She turned and ran, only to turn again, closer to the towering mast-ships.

"My lady, wait!"

She heard the man but didn't stop. When another sailor yelled at her, it fed her fear and she jumped off the dock to miss a barrel in her path. She slipped on landing but moved on, toward the ships. Her hair, once styled, held only with combs and pins, unraveled. Tendrils fell into her face, into her eyes. Behind her, the voices of her captors became more faint. She was moving quickly through the cargos and men, both of which increased in numbers closer to the ships. A group of men carrying freight, almost in a line, headed toward one ship and she darted on the far side of them, trying to hide from the upper docking. As they headed toward one gangway, she jumped onto the other. The dockworkers only gave her a glimpse. Amazed no one stopped her, she raced across the gangway.

One thing she hadn't counted on was the slippery wood of the walkway over the river. She slid onto the ship, tumbling forward, down and down into the bowels of the ship. Stunned, she tried to stop herself but soon slammed hard as she barreled into a wall of freight. Pain shot right through her again and everything went black.

C*LANK!*
The two straight swords rang loud, the vibration of the blow extended of the blade up James' arm. He grinned as Clearwater panted on his end, face red from the exertion of the sword practice.

"You realize this is just practice, do you not, Windhaven?" Clearwater spat out, withdrawing his sword from battle and wiping his upper lip with his shirtsleeve.

James chuckled. "Of course I do. More practice would aid your skill, verses cards and whores."

Clearwater smiled. "Ah, perhaps, but I believe my skill-set there is expertise, whereas you, my friend, would find yourself lacking." He cocked his head. "Marriage trapping you, ole man?"

"Happily so. An endeavor I trust you'll soon witness."

"Ah, yes, but that's where it all lies, isn't it?" Clearwater stretched his shoulders with a wince, almost making James laugh. The man was rusty in his fencing skills and stamina. "You, chap, married for love. Most of us do not favor that department as such. More of a need to save family fortunes and advance in the game—what lies in the best interest of all parties involved. Granted, I hope to like the future Countess of Clearwater, but lack of knowing or even liking a spouse is hardly a rule to prevent misguided marriages, as you are well aware of."

A servant approached with towels and a bowl of water for the lords to cool off with. Behind him was another who carried a tray of glasses, filled with water, wine, brandy and tea. James took a linen cloth and snatched a wine glass and downed a gulp of the madeira, enjoying the sweet, rich liquor bathe his throat. To his friend, he gave a nod and raised his glass.

"To the future Countess of Clearwater."

Clearwater snorted. "The lady of coin to save my soul," he said, raising his own acquired glass.

As both men drank to the future, boy raced into the hall of practice, skidding to a halt before them. James eyed the child. He appeared to be a young lad escaping the ruins of London's lower class area. His clothing was dirty, disheveled, and his sandy blonde hair flying wildly. The doorman followed, grabbing the boy by the scuff of his neck.

"Apologies, my lords." He turned on his heel, to drag the child away but the street urchin twisted and escaped.

"You lor' Windyhave?" he sputtered, panting.

James couldn't help but laugh. "I am Lord Windhaven."

The doorman reached for the boy again but the messenger withdrew a rolled note from his pocket, shoving it into James' hand. Puzzled, James raised his hand. "Let the child speak before you haul him off."

The doorman grumbled but stood back, his eyes never leaving the boy.

James opened the note, the words on it made him grit his teeth, his blood racing. "Where did you get this?"

"James, what does it say?" Clearwater threw his linen down and stepped closer.

"It says Eleanor was abducted," James said, his voice faded as the words crashed in.

A vision of his beautiful wife, her smile, in his mind's eye turned black when he thought of her bound and gagged. He shook off the image. Within a moment, he had the urchin's upper arms, raising him off the ground. "I said, how did you get this? Who sent you?"

The boy trembled. "Don't know, gov'na. Got it on the streets. Some bloke gave me coin to bring it."

James squeezed his hold tighter. "Who?"

"James, give the boy a moment." Clearwater tried to calm him with a quiet tone and hand on his arm. James didn't flinch.

"What were to do with the reply?"

"Don't rightly know, sur." The kid's eyes shifted away to the left, near the door. "Jus told to drop it to ya."

James blood boiled. He knew she shouldn't have gone.

"If the boy doesn't know, we need to find the carriage and the driver. He'd know." James strode to the bench, retrieving his hat and coat. "Need to get a party going, fan out to find her."

Clearwater followed after telling the servant to get the lad a bite. "Perhaps once he's filled, his tongue will be more lagging."

"We're already more than late." James gathered his horse's reins the moment he stepped outside the paddock.

"I need to find her—and the bastard who did this!"

Clearwater walked right behind James, but his eyes were still glued to the note. "It says you've got till morning to find twenty-thousand pounds sterling? Good grief! Who in the ton has that amount simply laying around to pay ransoms?"

James jaw twitched. He knew who had that kind of money, but hell would freeze before he gave it to him. The bastard would have him grovel for her. No, first James would do all he could to find his wife. He swung into the saddle and with a twist of the bridle ribbons, turned the equine around. "The bigger question is, where the hell is she? I swear, who ever harms her will pay. With his life! Ha!" He kneed the horse into a gallop down the village square.

He'd send his own search party out and find her before ever touching the coin. If anyone had hurt her, he'd kill them. Sending the horse galloping down the lane, his mind filled with images of Eleanor, the love of his life.

One thing was deadly accurate, to his way of thinking. He'd find her and then hunt down every man involved in this.

Eleanor....

Chapter Three

THE SLOSH OF THE OCEAN against the ship rocked the vessel ever so gently. It was a lure that kept her in the blissful moment of sleep she didn't want to surrender. But that peace was rudely interrupted by birds chirping loudly. Reluctantly, she tried to open her eyes but sleep called her to return.

She stretched, fitfully aware every limb was not bound and free to move, but they ached. Her head still pounded, pain started on top of her head and spread down to her shoulders, hips, arms and legs. In fact, her right arm throbbed more than the rest. As she propped herself up, she sat in a daze at what was around her. Above, mast sails billowed with the wind.

Slowly, she rose and instantly tilted on unsteady feet. A quick glance down, she saw her right foot was shoeless and her big toe peaking through a hole in her stocking. She looked for the missing shoe and found it just a few feet away. She put it on, and as she put her weight on it, she lost her balance again, the short heel broken off. Severely aggravated, she pulled off the other shoe and her stockings, since the one had been damaged. Now at least she'd have balance even though being barefoot during the daytime seemed out of place but she'd worry about that later.

With a sigh, she took in the state of her clothes. The silk empire gown had a tear down the right side and mud stains that marred the blue silk. Her pelisse was ripped straight down the back, making it a worthless piece. She yanked it off, not pleased to expose her neckline but the temperature of the air was warm enough she didn't miss the warmth the garment gave under normal circumstances. From the looks of her attire, and the touch of tendrils upon her cheek, she bet her hair was in disarray, too.

Confused as to where she was, she took a peek around the barrels in front of her. Crewmen were busy at work, moping the floor and moving supplies. They were dressed lightly, in only shirtsleeves and cotton pants that were cut just below their knees. And the most astounding thing to her was they were barefoot like her. She curled her toes. No wonder all she'd heard were voices and not boot heels on the wooden deck.

Around her immediate area were stacks of barrels and crates. For some reason, this looked familiar but she wasn't sure how. As she rubbed her arm, she tried to recall how. She was so lost in thought that when a man grabbed her arm, she jumped, a squeal escaping her lungs before she could stop it.

"Well, looky what I found, Norm!"

His grip on her was tight, but she stifled a whimper. She refused to let whoever they were know they caused her pain.

"Who might you be, pretty?"

She stared at the man. He was dressed as the rest, barefoot and loose-shirted. But his arm was like a rock, not moving. His hair was dirty, with half of the front in long, twirled locks, the rest pulled into a bandanna. The sailor gave her a half-grin. His brown eyes roved over her like a nobleman did upon buying a horse. But this one's smile revealed browned and broken teeth. The worst part was he stunk of onions and fish. Once more, her contents threatened.

"I'm…" She stopped, aware she didn't need to answer him.

The ugly sailor hadn't released her arm nor had he removed his gaze. His compatriot, another being desperately in need of a bath, stood next to the first, the look in his cloudy eyes told her more than she needed to know. He looked as if he was going to devour her. The thought made her stomach roll. She took a step back and her bare heel hit a crate.

"Sure as the day is long, you're a pretty piece of skirt," the second sailor drooled.

She swallowed. If she didn't do something, they'd have their way with her and that she couldn't have. "I request to see your captain. He is," she added, her mind racing, "expecting me."

The first man's eyebrows shot up. "Is he now?" He chuckled. "Well, wouldna want ta keep the man waitin'."

"I dunno. Bounty is shared here and as Is see it, she be plenty o' bounty." The second, shorter and wiry sailor reached to grab her skirt.

Appalled that they considered her a soiled dove, and that his filthy hand would clutch her silk dress, despite its ruined appearance, she gasped and tried to sidestep. But the first man's hold on her kept her from going far. If anything, he looked mad and glared at the other.

"You be lookin' to be whipped, are ya? If the cap't'n

wants her, he gets her. Afterward…" He winked.

Her mouth dropped at that appalling thought.

His friend opened his mouth, as if to protest, when the first elbowed his stomach. "Right on, Billy. We's be needin' to take 'er."

At least they'd let her get away from them and their lustful thoughts and for that she was grateful. The first man spun on his heel and started across the decking, dragging her with him, his fingers digging into her flesh. She winced in pain and was barely able to keep standing at the abruptness of his actions.

But as they stepped out onto the open deck, she tripped when her toe hit a board wrong. The one holding her kept her from hitting the planks, which she was somewhat thankful except his grip tightened harder, no doubt bruising her deep. The sea wind blew around them and up under her skirt, sending a chill to her bone, punctuating the danger around her. She noticed the scowls of the rough men directed at her and from a quick look around, realized she was the only woman there. An icicle shot down her spine. A scan of the horizon, looking for land and seeing only ocean, made the growing panic inside her double. She gulped. How was she to convince the captain to turn the ship around and return to the docks?

A flash of the docks raced through her head and something there made her more scared than the men glaring at her here. It was a memory that she tried to bring up but as she did, her head throbbed. Where was she? Who was she? The pain in her temple refused to let her think but a small voice deep inside laughed, telling her that the pain did not block her past and that scared her the most.

∞

Trent Cavendish stared at the maps on the desk, moving

the glass weight to another side to get a better view of the course he could steer the ship to. Gauging the weather, with the sun high, the current steady and prizes in reach, he tilted his head, waggle his lips at the mere suggestion of a successful day.

"Capt'n, I knows what your thinkin', but our letter of marque says—"

"I'm well aware of what that piece of scrawling says." His jaw ticked as his smile vanished. His quartermaster was too set to the rules—his mistake for enticing a law clerk to the account. With an inner sigh, he closed his eyes but for a moment. "Mr. Kendall, I remain captain of this ship not because of the good graces of the men out there, but because I can make them rich and feed their need for adventure. To remain bound to just French ships will sour their attitude, in which case I can lose my position." He bent forward on the table, hands balled into fists that supported him as he leaned across it, closer to the clerk-turned-quartermaster. "And may I remind you that if I lose mine, your position is also forfeit?"

Kendall's Adam's apple bobbed up and down as he swallowed, a noise that even he could hear. "Aye, sir." He swallowed again. "But captain, that's an English ship."

He leaned back against the table. "Perhaps."

Kendall's nerve came back. "You can't attack a British merchant ship. Those are our people. Not French, not even Spanish or Barbary pirates. You've no cause—"

"Aye, but I do have cause," he interrupted. "To the amount of sterling pounds. Cash, Mr. Kendall, and stores of profitable goods. The store on the *Angelina* is enough to make it worth our time and effort."

The quartermaster's face turned red in anger and his shoulders stiffened. It amused the captain, but only slightly. "But she's a British frigate."

"You do enjoy this life at sea, more than that tiny hole on Wharf Street I found you on, don't you, Mr. Kendall?"

That sort of comment always hit the mark. The man appeared to slump before him – only a minuscule amount but he noticed it. "Aye, sur."

He snorted. "Good. That is all." He waved the man off, wanting him gone before he truly throttled him for reminding him that all they had was the Regent's letter of marque to privateer against France, not raid treasures on any other ships. At the moment, one of those other ships commanded his attention and he returned to the map before him with the trajectory of the *Angelina* configured.

The door to his cabin burst open.

"Capt'n!"

Before him, two of his men stumbled into the room, their hands holding a woman's arms. She fell down, dragging Norm with her.

"Billy, whatever are you doing?" Where the hell had a woman come from? No doubt, one of the men snuck her aboard for whatever reason, though he could guess what. Or worse, she was a runaway who stole aboard to escape whatever issue plagued her—prostitution, irate father, poverty, drunkard, or many more excuses.

"Found 'er in the hold, sir, hidin'," the taller, bulkier pirate sputtered.

He gave her a look-over, a little deeper than previous. She was petite just in comparing her size to Norm, who was one of the shorter pirates aboard the *Equuleus's* crew. Definitely young, her skin was ivory white and her golden sable mane looked as if it had been coiffed up at one point during her voyage, but now, long locks of curls escaped the few hairpins' hold. Her gown, a striped blue and white garment, held tears and stains of a harsh life but it's silk material made him wonder if she wasn't some kept cour-

tesan with a brutal lover she escaped from. Her brilliant
blue sapphire eyes stared at him with no hesitation or fear,
which surprised him and instantly made him decide she
must be a runaway. With a deep inner breath, he would
have to correct her plans, for stealing onto a pirate ship
was the worst choice a woman could make.

"Who might I be addressing here? Miss....?"

His addressing her seemed to snap her into her position
now and she struggle to free herself of the two men. He
motioned to them to let her go and once they did, she
bounced to her feet—her bare feet.

She stood, glaring at him, anger and frustration reflected
in her gaze but somehow, he didn't think it was necessarily at him. If nothing more, his attraction to this waif
was growing, for she didn't appear the slightest concern at
being on a pirate ship.

"The question, dear captain, should be who are you?"
She glanced back at her escorts. "To call me to your ship,
only to throw me into the grasp of your underlings."

He couldn't help but smile at her statement, one that set
Norm and Billy into a bickering state, that they'd done
nothing amiss. Catching Billy's attention, he said, "Go."

The two scurried out the door, shutting it behind them.
Now, he could concentrate on her and that would only
be brief. Despite her beauty, he had a prize to capture so
he needed to return to his plans. He turned, grabbed a
cup from his desk and poured from the bottle sitting on
top of the table.

"This should calm your humors." He shoved the cup
into her dainty hand, taking into account how she del-
icately gripped the cup handle, as if it were crafted of
fine imported china, instead of West Indies crockery. That
gesture made him reassess his view on her, because that
was the way of a lady. Perhaps the courtesan runaway was

closer to the mark.

She took a sip and nearly sputtered. "That is not wine, sir."

He chuckled. "No, it isn't. It's rum, from one of the finest plantations in the Indies." He paused. "To whom do I have the pleasure of sailing with, my lady?"

The question and specifically his calling her lady, got a response. She stood straighter, her chin raised, but in seconds, a puzzled look flashed in her eyes and she bit her bottom lip.

"I believe you owe me an introduction first, sir."

He snorted. "I'm Captain Trenton Cavendish of the *Equuleus*."

∞

SHE STILL FELT THE BURN down her throat from the rum and the warmth that spread from her belly throughout her body in reaction to the liquor. That feeling helped to calm her frayed nerves, ones so disjointed that she took another sip, slowly, as she studied the man before her.

Her mind was a muddled mess. The ache wasn't as bad, perhaps the rum helped on that, but there was a blank spot in her thinking. Who was she? How did she get here? How did she answer his question when this place reeked of a prison for her, surrounded by water and men? She swallowed.

Cavendish offered her a chair in silence, as if offering her a seat would jog her memory. She took the chance to sit, still trying to find something useful to answer him with. How did she not recall her name? She went to take another sip.

"Whoa, I'd take it easy on that, my lady." He laughed.

She peered at him from the rim of the cup. Cavendish

was a very handsome man, in a very rugged sort of way. Even leaning back, so casually, he was a tall, broad-shouldered man dressed in a loose linen shirt. His bulky upper arms filled the shirt sleeves, leaving her imagine muscles that'd twitch with any movement. The shirt was tucked at his narrow waist into the top of dark-colored breeches, the color muted by numerous wearings, just like his leather boots, creased with history.

Realizing she just looked him over, a blush heated her cheeks and humor danced in his eyes, no doubt from catching her stare. Those eyes were warm and enticing walnut shade, sparkling even now with mischief. His face was tanned by the sun, just like the rest of his exposed skin and she wondered where else. The man cocked his head, making a loose stand of hair fall across his forehead, and exposed the gold hoop on his ear that gleamed from the sunlight streaming in through the dirty window.

The jewelry made her pause. Men did not wear earrings except, she'd once heard, pirates. Her heart skipped a beat. Pirates? She blinked hard. It must be the rum.

"I am…" She stopped. Nothing came. All seemed blank and her temple throbbed. She pushed her fingers against it.

Cavendish's brows furrowed. He took the cup from her and tilted her chin up toward him, her hand falling to her side. With a gentleness she didn't expect from a man as big as him, he turned her head from side to side slowly.

"Do you remember how you got on my ship?"

She bit her bottom lip again. "No," she whispered.

He hummed. "You've got a bruise on your cheek and one close to where you were rubbing. Do you hurt anywhere else?"

She nodded, her eyes filling with tears. It was as if a wall had been built in her head, blocking her memory and she could not seem to find the door to open it. Frustration and pain were building inside her and she wanted to scream.

"You have no recall on who you might be?"

Through blurred eyes, she tried to see him. "No." She pulled her chin from his touch, despite the warmth and the faint hint of security it gave, something that might have made her concerned if it weren't for her loss memory.

"I believe you must of fallen during your descent to the ship. The loss of self may come from this bruise upon your head. I will send you to the ship's surgeon. Perhaps he'll know what to do." He took her arm to help her up.

Biting back the tears, she nodded. "Thank you."

He chuckled. "Don't thank me yet. The *Equuleus* is not a safe place, my lady. But we will see what we can do."

The odd sense of security came sweeping back to her as her hand rested on his arm. Those tightly woven muscles did twitch at her touch, just as she knew they would. It was a strange thought to have, but surprising how it comforted her. She leaned a little more towards Cavendish without falling into him, suddenly feeling that every one of her limbs ached with a couple areas like her thigh and feet hurt.

He deposited her in the surgeon's lair, gave the man strict instructions to mend her pains, and then he left as if a tempest chased him. If her head didn't hurt, she might have asked him why.

Chapter Four

THE SEARCH FOR ELEANOR DIDN'T take James long to organize. Originally, his only thought was to mount his best stallion and run the area himself, but Clearwater persuaded him to find more men.

"We can spread out," his friend argued. "Cover more ground." His voice dropped. "And let you concentrate on who might demand such a price and how you might raise it so fast."

Twenty thousand pounds sterling… It was a king's ransom from the standpoint that most noblemen did not have that amount available in cash. James could easily count who needed that sort of sum, hence marriages with wealthy families that could curtail debt collectors. That thought made him flip to another thought. Who did he know that was that far into arrears?

The answer startled him. Not as many as he thought. In fact, he didn't know any, but then again, most hid their debts. Unable to clear his mind of anything other than Eleanor, he summoned his staff, putting the stable boys and his able servants onto the team and pulled maps out, directing them toward different sections to search. He and Clearwater took the roadway she would've taken.

What would he do without his Eleanor?

TRENT STORMED ONTO THE UPPER deck, anger flooding his veins.

"What's got you going? We'd be at sea or I'd be betting a bee in your hat 'cept you ain't wearin' one."

He shot a look at the first mate, Fitzgibbons. The man had the audacity to be smiling at him and that irritated Trent that much more.

"Stop before you say another word that'll get your Irish arse thrown over the railing." The threat wouldn't work. Fitzgibbons had goaded Trent every day on this trip, why stop now?

The Irishman leaned on the railing over the deck, not the one Trent had threatened him with, his head cocked to the side. "Heard a lass was found below. Thought you told the boys not to be bringin' a whore with them."

"She's not a lady of ill-repute, but yes, found below. Apparently not a stowaway, either. She fell, as it were, into the hold, banged her head something fierce and now has no recall who she is or how she ended up here." He spat over the side of the ship.

"Aye, so I see."

Trent frowned. "Whatever thought you have, erase it. The *Prestige* is up ahead. We got work to do."

"When will you give up and seek the ass out in a duel, like proper lads should?"

He closed his eyes. A duel? Revenge turned cold at such civilized rituals and he'd sworn revenge.

"You know I left 'proper' long ago."

The man shrugged. "So why are you so mad?"

"There's a woman aboard," he hissed.

"And the crew will be pleased. A dessert, do ya not think, ta taking the prize?"

"She isn't a whore!" Trent's nightmare grew. Of course, the crew would love to share a prize like her. And it might distract them from asking like why attack a British merchantman when there were bigger ships with better hauls? "She's a lady, one who needs to be protected, not ravaged."

He pushed down the image that kept trying to appear in his head. When he first learned of the girl, he had been slightly amused but soon turned annoyed and as the thought lingered, anger took hold.

"A proper lady on board, with all the airs o' privilege, reminds you o' Rachel, doesn't she, lad?" The first mate's voice was barely audible but it spoke volumes.

Being caught in this dilemma, feeling the swell in his heart before it plummeted to his stomach, was dead-on what had set the anger off. *Dear Rachel!* His wife was the last woman on this ship; the last woman he had embraced. He loved her and as her husband, he was to protect her and it's the one thing he failed at doing. That fact ate at him every moment of every day, and fueled him for revenge. And now this lady appeared, on his ship no less, and all the memories of Rachel exploded in his head. No, that wasn't entirely true. What bothered him was this lady was beauty in a world of hate he had contrived and her beauty begged at a need, a desire he thought had died with Rachel. That disturbed him the most. He was to honor his wife but found his cock tightened, even now, in response to her. He found he couldn't wait to get rid of her, because she woke remembrances that were better left buried.

"You did tha' best ya could, Capt'n. Never forget that."

"I swore I'd find the man responsible for her death and grant him the same concession, so no, she'll never be forgotten." He swallowed the sour taste of loss and anger that brewed. Steeling his shoulders, he pulled the scope up and peered through the lenses. "That ship still hasn't detected we plan to take her." He smiled.

"Well, why would she? We bear colors that donna resemble the black."

Trent couldn't hide the smile. No, the *Prestige* would remain clueless to his approach until it was too late. Rachel's revenge was getting closer.

T HE SHIP'S SURGEON WAS NOTHING more than a prying, probing demon, one that at first made her shirk his touch out of what seemed to her to be impropriety, to his ministrations making her angry. The man knew nothing of the healing arts, she decided, but only specialized in mortal wounds from the looks of his cutting instruments. The faster she could to escape him and his sharp tools, the better. All he did was tell her what she already knew—the bump on her head not only hurt but scrambled her memory to hither and yond. Her hands clenched, her short nails digging into her palms as he touched her, ostensible to check her temple but the closeness, the smell of his foul breath and the presence of him as a man stirred a vision in her mind of two other rapscallions who had hit her in the first place. That memory made her freeze as all her thoughts turned to escaping this torture. And when the surgeon bent to pick up some odd looking tool off his table, she bolted past him, though the couple men who accidently stood in her path and flew up the ladder, each one hitting a pain point that riveted through her but she had to flee.

As she stepped out onto the wooden deck, the dampness seeped into the soles of her bare feet. The sun drenched the boat and its heat was welcomed. She inhaled the salt-air and found it refreshing which surprised her as she'd never been on the seas and rarely ever in town near the docks. She stood, basking in the sunlight and even shook her head a smidgen, making her hair brush her shoulders and back. While the ship's doctor rambled, searching his tonics in theory for something for her, she simply pulled the hairpins out as best she could, pocketing the pins.

One of the ship's crewman came to a screeching halt before her, sliding to a stop barely in time. She hadn't seen him coming and at the vision of being run into, she stepped back, her own footing wanting to give. She reached for a railing or something to keep her from falling again, though this time straight on her bottom, and the only thing available was his arms. A gasp escaped her lips.

"Oh! For the Saints! 'Scuse me, missy!"

Shocked, she stood wide-eyed, taking in how he barely looked old enough to reach over the railing, not as a member of the crew. Her heart thudded widely after it skipped a beat when he virtually knocked her down. Still shaken, she could barely breath when he took off.

As if in a bad dream, she watched the scene before her unfold as if she'd walked into a tempest. The men, really boys, were not just doing chores but something more. Above her, the sails to the ship unfurled, catching the wind to drive her forward through the waves. Voices yelled back and forth as men climbed the rigging and others prepared below by clearing the decking. Stunned, she didn't move except when another man repeated the first by almost running into her.

The second near mishap with one of the men was followed by another crash across deck, then another. It took a moment for it to register but her skin prickled and turned hotter than just from the sun and the warmth of the day. No, it was generated by the heat of the growing number of eyes that stared at her. Fear snaked down her spine, escalating as another thud followed by curses filled the air. Once she figured out she was the cause of their mishaps, she turned to retreat the way she came when she came abruptly to a halt from the man who appeared out of no where before her.

"What in the name of St. Peter are you doing out here!"

It was a statement that was a question, a vulgarity she did not deserve except the voice was deep, masculine and alluring. The captain...

One thing was for sure. Despite ruggedly handsome, he was mad. If nothing else, he glowed with authority and his presence made her insides burn with an attraction she couldn't stop. She bit her bottom lip and refused to look away though there was fire in his eyes, one lit because of something she did? Her nostrils flared, inhaling the scent that was him, all male and untainted by the sweetness of the men she knew. That thought made her wonder, as she shivered before him, who were the men she knew?

"I stayed with that surgeon long enough. He has no training for the medical arts. In fact, he was..." She paused, her blood curdling at the memory of his filthy hands touching her.

"His primary station is to tend to my men, not cater to the ladies," he snapped back. "But he has the manners to know better than let any woman of quality venture onto a deck alone."

"How dare you imply I am not a lady of quality!"

He stepped closer, his shoulders tense, jaw tight. "So memory returns. Who are you?"

She frowned, aggravated beyond reason. "No, I still do

not recall. But I do know that I am of station, one you should heed to."

In a swift moment, he snorted, the hint of a grin on his lips but his hand clamped around her arm and spun her around. She winced as his fingers dug into her and knew she'd see the marks later. How dare he! She was about to lodge her complaint but the wind sucked the words out of her mouth as he led her across the decking, barking orders at his men who stood motionless, watching them.

Did he order them to prepare the guns?

What had she fallen into?

☾☽

TRENT STEERED HER TO HIS cabin, his mind racing. His men had stopped preparations when they spotted the girl standing on deck, most of them staring as if she was a siren, luring them to her. He had no choice but to scoop her away and stick her in his cabin, away from them and from the upcoming battle. He'd hoped Doc had kept her under his watch but the surgeon had sent word that she stopped his exam, accusing him of inept skills and stormed out, which he did not stop because he would not keep watch on an insulting, overbearing woman who thought to highly of herself, memory or not. Therefor, with a growl, Trent had to take matters into his own hands and that irritated him to no end. His mind sat to hunt and take his prize, not deal with a delicate lady who needed protection against his men, against the dangers of the upcoming battle and against him.

The last thought brought his rapid stride to a halt. Thankfully it was at the cabin door but still, where had that come from?

His abrupt stop caused her bump right into him. He felt every last inch of her against him—her breasts, even encumbered in stays and a bodice, her quivering belly, the soft and warm touch of her breath against his neck and the impact of her legs hitting the backs of his thighs sent a lightning bolt of fire spiraling down below his belt. It was the last thing he needed, to feel any compassion for her because that often turned to more and that he would not allow. But at the moment, he could only blame himself for her slamming into him. Damn!

With more force than necessary, he threw the door open and whirled her inside the cabin before him. The gasp that escaped her mouth at his fast maneuvering grated on him, recalling his mother's schooling on how to respect the fairer sex. Well, this member of that class made herself part of his concern and that wasn't good, considering this was a pirate ship.

She caught herself from falling as he released his grip once she was inside. With a quick spin on her heel, she faced him, her cheeks reddening and her eyes blazing.

"How dare you handle me as if I was no better than a lady of ill-repute! I am Lady…" Her angered tongue silenced. The look she had appeared as if the wheels of a windmill were spinning, trying to engage a mill to work on its power but it faded as her lips thinned. "I'm a noble lady, one to be given much respect…"

He snorted. "I've given you respect and more but let me clarify this for you." He stepped closer to her, not sure why. Perhaps it was to bask in her beauty and inhale the fresh scent she wore like a skin, a touch of lavender so sweet it ate at his soul. He inhaled it, which only fueled the fire in his loins. "You're not on a passenger ship. This is the type of vessel that the men either fear the bad luck you'd bring, being a woman, and the other set would rather take carnal knowledge. You will stay here. That is an order."

She blinked in disbelief. He expected that.

"How dare you!" The words spilled from her mouth and instantly, he saw her retract, as if she realized she was not among an equal.

"You will do as I command. I have business here first, then we can discuss how to handle your affectation."

Those beautiful golden brows furrowed. "What business?"

He didn't answer. How could he? He needed his mission to remain unknown to her, for once he could return her to some port, she became a liability to this ship if she knew the truth.

Her gaze narrowed and her jaw tightened upon his pause. "What style of business? I heard words spoken by your men of guns and tightening the sails. Even though I may not fathom how sails are with this, guns are rather specific, wouldn't you say?"

"You are quite outspoken for a fine lady." He really had no time for this. "We are at war. Sailing requires guns to journey out of England, even for merchant ships." That was a lie but one a woman at her station in the peerage wouldn't have knowledge of. "There is a ship of unknown origins in our path. I will not risk losing my crew, nor my guest, nor my ship to the enemy. So," he took another step closer to her, reaching for her arms to keep her still, "you will remain here. For your safety," he added.

Confusion swirled in her gorgeous blue eyes. Perhaps she was a siren, one that held the beauty of Aphrodite and the countenance of a lady. Who was she?

The vision of the siren struggled in his grasp, her eyes widening with fear or mystery, he wasn't sure. She opened her mouth but Trent, lured by, felt his control over the beast inside failed, and he pulled her to his chest. The flame ignited by touching her jolted him, awakening a passion he'd thought long dead. Instantly, his body tightened. Before he knew what he was doing, his mouth sealed hers, kissing her deeply.

At that moment, he lost himself.

Chapter Five

"GEORGE, WHAT HAPPENED?" JAMES STARED at his carriage driver, biting back accusatory words and expletives for losing the woman he loved. He was exhausted, working with little sleep, without much food as he pushed himself harder to find Eleanor.

George hacked. Partially propped up on the bed, his battered body bandaged, his broken arm bound with wood slats, the man was barely able to look at him through his only open eye, the other badly swollen shut, black and bruised.

"We were attacked, near Brightiron. I think," he sputtered and stopped. James picked up the cup of water and gently tipped it towards the servant's lips. He took a sip and pulled back. "I think it was three highway men, my lord. That was all I could tell."

"And Lady Eleanor?" He hung on a loose thread, hoping something would spill from the man but the George's wife, who stood to the side, glared at James, warning him to stop. To hell with her! He needed more!

George frowned, his look puzzled. "My lord, they

seemed more interested in taking her than stealing gems or anything of monetary value."

With a huff of disgust, James paced, trying to prevent his hands from clenching. This was his trusted servant, not the enemy to strike. He refocused on Eleanor.

"Did they say anything at all that might strike a light? Like where would they take her or for whom? Any tracks of their departure the rains washed away."

The injured man shook his head for a second. "No, sir. But their abduction of Lady Eleanor…" His voice faded as he made motions to his wife. With noticeable reluctance, his wife grabbed a stained coat off the table and brought it to him. George fumbled with the coat's pocket and with an unsteady hand, withdrew a scrap of paper.

James snatched the piece and tipped it toward the firelight to see the faint writing on it.

"Dryer's." He frowned. The name didn't hold much meaning. Was it the abductor's? Where they planned to take her? He needed more. "Where the bloody-sakes is this?" he snapped at his servant and nearly bit his tongue, realizing he was yelling at an injured man.

"The wharf, my lord," George answered, his voice shaky. "I've heard the name in regards to a warehouse of that name. My brother, Howard, works along the Thames, hauling cargo. He spoke of it in the past."

For once, he had a piece of information that might lead to an end. Inside, his heart leapt with hope and started thudding with excitement. He wanted to race to the docks immediately, but the dusky skies outside hindered his enthusiasm. A plan. He needed to devise a plan and gather men. The docks, particularly at night, were not safe and if Eleanor was there, he must waste no time, but endangering her life without thought he could not do.

He glanced down at his servant. "Godspeed in your

recovery, George. Her ladyship will require your services, upon her return." He smiled and took off, rather pleased to have a positive outlook for once.

Now, the once dead-end turned to life and he wanted to sing. *Eleanor, my love, I will see you soon!*

❧

THE ENTIRE SHIP RATTLED AND shook again, compounded by a loud, piercing explosion. She tightened her grip on around her knees as she squeezed into a ball on the floor near the bed. She'd tried sitting on the bed, in the chair, under the desk and in the corner only to feel every impact of the blasts against the ship reverberate through her bones. She'd shrieked at first, just out of shock and being scared out of her mind but she learned to control herself. Prayer would serve a better purpose and she began the Lord's Prayer when another explosion slammed into the ship. She shut her eyes, reciting the prayer as she rocked back and forth.

The sounds of the men mixed with the gun blasts. A creak of wood resounded as well as the ship listing to one side. Frankly, she was shocked the ocean hadn't invaded through the walls but she bit her tongue from voicing out loud that fear, for what if the fates turned their back to her and let the waves in.

The noise of the attack—though to be honest, she wasn't sure who attacked who first—increased another note, as if the ships were side by side. Unable to contain herself, she leapt and ran to the porthole, taking a short glance outside. The minute she stood there told her more than she wanted and she wished she hadn't gone.

The other ship flew the British Union Jack. She frowned. The captain had stated there was a war going on, one her addled brain couldn't recall, but if the ship she was on was

English, why would they attack another British ship?

Her curiosity peaked at that question and gave her the bravery to stand, despite the shaking of the floorboards and rattling of the walls. Tiny steps were all that was needed to cross the small cabin room to the door and bracing herself against the backside of it, she creaked it open just enough to peek out. She wasn't ready for the scene before her.

Smoke filled the air despite the wind that worked furiously to dissipate it. The deck was wet with seawater and traces of blood. Barefooted sailors scurried across the deck, working to control the riggings, one of which had been severed by a cannonball, others working on the guns on the starboard side of the ship. The screams of the injured pierced the air, mixed with the yelling of commands. It was exciting and terrifying all at once, stirring her heart into a rapid beat that made the air thick to breath.

She glanced up the mast to the flag that whipped in the wind, fully expecting an Union Jack to be there, just like the other vessel, but what she saw took the rest of her breath away—a black flag. Pirates! Her heart even skipped a beat at the thought and she lowered her gaze to the high deck just beyond the mast and found Captain Cavendish there, looking glass in hand. She frowned. The idea of piracy didn't make sense. He had the manners, though rusty, of a gentleman, having seen to her needs and welfare. His mastery of the English language equaled that of her peers, a thought that hinged at her memory though nothing more came. No, her mind was buzzing. He talked succinctly, she caught glimpses of the others that didn't, though she'd guess sailing outside His Majesty's Royal Navy didn't attract the most educated men. He gave the airs of a gentleman. Pirates didn't do that...or did they?

As another boom rattled the ship, she retreated to the corner of the room, sitting on the floor. Her mind was

muddled and her head hurt, each explosion only inten-
sified the pain in her temples. She pulled her knees up,
cradling her legs close and lowered her head, fear slither-
ing down her spine that she'd escaped those demons that
hunted her only to now be killed at sea aboard a pirate
ship. She wanted to scream.

∞

FINALLY THE SHIPS WERE CLOSE enough that Trent
ordered the boarding planks lowered, connecting the
two ships.

He crossed the plank onto the *Prestige*, jumping off
it and hitting the deck with his boot heels, the sound
reverberating. Before him stood the merchantman's crew,
made up mostly of young lads, barely able to walk. Trent
inwardly winced. Hadn't he, himself, stowed away on a
tug when he was barely in britches? The call of the sea
pulling him toward to take sail? He shook his head and
refocused. The captain was near the mainmast, with one
of Trent's men nearby, pistol in hand and cutlass in his belt.

The captain's neutral expression didn't surprise Trent.
The man had seen the black flag and felt the fury of cannon fire warning of their approach The fact that he'd
surrendered his ship so easily did pique Trent's attention.
To relinquish a ship was not easy as ships were the life-
blood of the seas. This man didn't even try to outrun
them. Trying to school his own surprise, Trent went over
to the captured man and cocked his head.

"So easy to quit, are we?"

The captain shifted on his feet, his brows fretting. "You
swayed colors as British ship to turn fire on us, raising the
black instead. Your guns outnumber mine as I'm only a
merchant ship."

Trent snorted, one side of his mouth curling up in a

lopsided grin, a grin that went no further than that. "I swing the colors that will get me what I want, Captain..."

The man grimaced. "Captain Burrows of the *Prestige*."

"Yes. Is this ship not of the Kensington fleet? Shipping goods through troubled waters from India and further places of the Far East."

Burrows eyes narrowed. "Yes, you designate us right."

Now Trent smiled. "Excellent. Men!" Behind him, most of the men scurried to the lower decks to the ship's hold, leaving an armed set above to keep guard on the crew. Trent's prize, though, did not sit below, but here. "Captain, I must see your manifest and log."

Burrows grumbled low. "It will tell you nothing more than what I hold below."

"Perhaps. But I am interested in the past shipments." His hand went to rest on the hilt of his sword, tucked into his belt. As Burrows mumbled, Trent paid no mind as he followed the man back to the captain's cabin.

This ship, sailing under the banners of Kensington, held a far greater prize in the captain's log and that made Trent's blood race with excitement. His revenge drew closer.

Chapter Six

SHE COUNTED IN HER HEAD. This time, she reached one hundred. During that space, there was no more blasts, no more yelling of orders. Nor was there the stench of sulfur, seawater, or men screaming from injuries. In fact, it was quiet, way too quiet. The type of silence that was deafening.

Slowly she raised her head off her knees and stood up. Her temple throbbed and a quick touch brought not only pain but surprise as the spot was swollen and hot. The pain at least reminded her she was alive and survived the attack. A quick look showed the cabin survived too but what about the rest of the ship? She peered out the port-hole to find the whole decking appeared in good shape but absent most of the pirates. She frowned, curious, until she looked right and found the shredded sail of another ship that was extremely close. The ship they had taken. She shuttered at the thought. The decking she stood on belonged to pirates and she'd best remember that.

The realization hit her deep. Pirates. Would she survive? Did she have a choice? Another pang came to her belly and this one she recognized clearly. It shouted hunger. She tried to find a clue as to the last time she ate anything but the blackness in her memory yielded nothing. A glance around the captain's quarters gave no glimpse of food. Now what was she to do? She was tired of trying to get her memory to work. Whatever happened to cause it to vacate her must have been terrible. The soft swelling and shooting pain on her head verified that. How she got onto a pirate ship was also beyond her recall. But hunger now took control and she needed to find something or pass out.

As she spun on her heels to leave and demand something to eat, she spied a looking glass above the chest to the side of the small room. How she'd missed it before, she didn't know. A quick look showed just how totally disheveled she was. She frowned. A lady. Without knowing more, she did know she was of better quality than the rapscallions aboard this ship. But she was a mess. The cabin surely had other clothes in it, no doubt for him, but he could share, she decided. Over on the wall, near the looking glass, were two linen shirts hanging from pegs and a pair of trousers. She yanked them off the hooks and, after a quick look to make sure the door was closed and the sound of silence still reigned, she pulled the tattered dress off and shrugged the shirt over her head. It billowed above her knees. The coarse linen pants were way too big and fell to her ankles but she didn't care. Snagging the rope that kept the chest secured to the wall, she tied it about her waist to keep the pants up. Instantly, she felt more covered than when wearing the dress.

Another glance into the glass reminded her she wasn't finished. With a quick yank, she freed her mane and she used her fingers to loosen the tangles. Pulling it all up into a knot in the back of her head, she pinned it in place. It wasn't perfect, but it would do. She plucked up a hat on the back of his desk chair. It was a big brown felt piece, worn and floppy. Jamming it on her head transformed her from the lady without a home to a pirate look–alike.

Pleased with herself, she padded to the door and inched it open. Two sailors nearby busily coiled rope. Neither glanced at her. Elated they ignored her, she stepped onto the deck and scanned the horizon before her. Captain Cavendish talked to another man on the other ship. Various crewmen milled about, piling goods near the plank that took them back to the *Equuleus*. Standing still, she inhaled the fresh air, the scent of sea mixed with gun smoke easily tasted. Which made her stomach growl again. The sound was loud, though no eyes turned toward her.

"Aye there, lassie!" The thick Irish brogue whispered in her ear and she jumped. "If I were ya, I'd refrain meself," he added.

With a gulp, she stared at the sailor next to her. Big and bulky, he stood, with his hair pulled back in a queue and laugh lines etched near his eyes. His gaze roved down her in her borrowed clothes and instantly she cringed, her cheeks turning hot as she no doubt was blushing and her toes curled, as if to try and hide. The billowy shirt hid her narrow waist and her breasts but if the wind blew wrong, too much would be displayed. She swallowed her fear, straightened her shoulders and lifted her chin as she returned the look. Hunger pushed her to be forward. That was the excuse she'd use, unless she really was so bold. But he grinned at her, and that made her determination to find food return in full force.

"Pardon me," she replied. "I'm simply too hungry to keep hid till whenever Captain Cavendish returned." She hoped that sounded proper enough, though why on this ship she cared was beyond her reasoning.

"Hungry, are we? And the capt'n didna have you fed?" At her negative shake, the man grabbed her hand. "Well, let me see if I canna help you. I'm First Mate Fitzgibbons, at yer service." He tipped his head.

For once, manners! She smiled. "Nice to meet you, especially if you can help me find the kitchen." She bit back saying she couldn't recall who she was.

"Ya, lassie, here it'd be called the galley." He chuckled, obviously ignoring her lack of name.

"Wonderful! Would you please be so inclined to put me in the right direction? I fear if I don't have a nibble, I may fall."

His grin slightly faded as he took in the decking and across to the other side. No one had noticed her yet but a clutch of pirates were returning, rolling barrels across the plank,.

The first mate took her hand and spun her about. "I believe it would be best if'n I fetch ya a few morsels without notice." He took her to the side of the ship away from the crossing planks to a bench surrounding the hold. He sat her down there. "Shove that hat down missy and dunna think of gittin' up. I'll be back right soon."

She'd do whatever he said if he brought her food. With a nod, she startled when his hand squeezed hers before he set off. She tried not to think too much into it. Apparently, he was not like his men, who held the superstition that she, as a woman aboard, was bad luck. Not that she had made a beeline for this ship, that she was sure of. Out of a veiled memory, a muted scene of her flying through the boardwalk near the water, her terror stalking her every move. A single leap onto a ladder that lead upward to the docks and running upon a wet wooden plank crept into her mind. Excited at the hint of her past and scared by what she saw, she said nothing and then her stomach growled. Food—how she needed some for without it, she would no doubt act rashly and that could work against her present condition.

The sun beat down on the ship and the heat warmed her. The coolness of earlier, from winds bracing across the deck, dissipated under the heat of the rays. With the hat on her head, she didn't feel cooked. A slight breeze wisped against her and the combination rejuvenated her. And when the Irishman returned, shoving a small bowl filled with some stew and a lump of bread, she wanted to sing. Instead she took a large bite of the bread after dipping it in the bowl and the man laughed.

"May I request a spoon from you?"

Fitzgibbons laughed. "That, my dear, is wha' the bread be for." He sat a mug beside her as she made another swipe in the bowl. "Here, a mug of wine. Now it ain't the type you be use to, but its all we got." He winked.

Pulling the tankard up, she could smell the red wine before the first swallow. It was no better than she'd thought so for this place. It was slightly off taste, overly bitter, but it burned its way down, quenching her thirst.

"Thank you."

He nodded and walked away.

Quietly, she ate, keeping an eye on all she could see. The first set of pirates returned with barrels that they took to the hold. More crossed the bridge. Cavendish wasn't one of them. In fact, she couldn't find him any more on the other ship nor on this one. It unsettled her and that made her confused. The man had left her starving, scared to leave his cabin for fear of her life but now she wanted him back?

No one had gazed in her direction. Perhaps the outfit worked. She prayed it did. As she finished the last of the stew and swallowed the bitter wine till the cup was empty, she stood. More pirates returned, not all carrying goods from the ship. The confidence she had fled as they walked over the bridge, making her long to be in those quarters.

Mr. Fitzgibbons stood near the planks, writing in a ledger, and he glanced at her. He gave her a brief nod. It was a message that he'd watch over her if she wished to stay. She gave him a shy smile and with a small sigh, closed her eyes.

The sounds of the ocean currents sloshing against the boat, the rocking of the ship lulled her to ease. For once, the fatigue of everything was inching into her soul. Nothing was normal for her. But until she could get a foothold on where she was, who she was, nothing was right. What she witnessed in the attack on the British ship was wrong. Being on this vessel wasn't her. These clothes were definitely not her style. If she could just rest, perhaps it would fall into place...

The men below in the hold spoke in English but with a few words she didn't understand. It made the speech sing-song, like a bird. Yet a word broke through that wasn't. The tone also changed. It was in Spanish. She tilted her head but kept her eyes closed, listening. The words came to her, and her mind translated them.

"Once more, we strike for a prize that falls too short of reward."

"Yes, but he'll claim it was worth far more, mark my words," the other pirate retorted.

"Last haul, we gained but handful of wealth that lasted only one day at port." the first one spat. *"In the name of God above, I will not fall that far short again."*

There was a rustling she heard, like they were rummaging through a box of metal pieces. Her mind put silver pitchers and serving pieces in it and she laughed inwardly. What would pirates want of a tea set?

"Carlos, this box has far more worth than the rest," came the

excited pirate. "I refuse to share this," he added with a snarl.

"Pedro, I have found more trinkets…" his friend murmured. "No one knows we have these. The crates marked them as tools."

Carlos laughed low and sinisterly. "Then let us replace just items with tools…"

A loud splash against the boat underneath her drowned out their voices and her eyes snapped open. She strained to hear more but could not through the waves and the sound of more men returning. Without actually bending forward, she tried to peer down into the hold for a look at the culprits who plotted to steal from Cavendish, who stole from the ship across the way. But her eyes couldn't adjust from being shut to pure sunlight.

"What, may I ask, do you think you're doing out here?" The voice was deep, sensual and made her jump, which caused her hat to fall and the cascade of curls fell from wayward pins. Fear raced through her.

Cavendish stood before, fire in his eyes, his legs planted like trees, unmoving and his arms akimbo. "Speak, before I throw you to the sharks and rid my ship of bad luck."

She gasped.

SINCE WHEN DID HE THREATEN women? Especially ladies? He could faintly hear his mother's voice, a woman long since gone from this world, admonishing him for speaking such words to this waif dressed in men's clothing. Correction—dressed in his clothing. His emotions were a mixture of disbelief, amusement, irritation, and attraction all whirling inside him. Particularly how the oversized shirt and loose pants seemed to enhance her beauty, tugging at the carnal beast inside him that he believed long dead and dormant. The linen cloth, especially with the neckline, gave hints of a cleavage and breasts beneath it. No doubt her nipples would have shown through the loose weave but since they didn't, he could only imagine she still wore her stays. Pity... The pants, larger than her body's size, bound by rope at her narrow waist, only enticed him to imagine the shapely form beneath the material. Fire sparked in his loins and grew with each second she stood before him. His cock thickened, the hardness forming only reminded him it'd been too long. He tightened and that set off a new round of emotions inside him in reaction to this need that brewed deep.

Irritation at her grew exponentially. The finale blurt of how the sharks would rid him of an evil spewed out of his lips before he thought clearly. Damn! Even now, her eyes were wide open and her upper lip trembled. It was a mistake to notice because he now saw the bread crumb that had remained on her rosy-hinted lip. The piece beckoned to him to invade her mouth, a mouth framed in soft flesh, the type he'd seal his own to....

The fire inside him inched another notch hotter. His cock stirred, stiffening at the mere suggestion of her clad in clothes that could easily be ripped off. His mouth dried. He hadn't felt this way since Rachel. Memory of his wife should've shunted his attraction to the lass immediately, as it had for the last dozen women, ladies to strumpets, who had tried to seduce him. But this woman didn't. In fact, she stirred his body to life.

With a growl, he grabbed her wrist and yanked her to her feet as he turned to take her away from the deck, where prying eyes witnessed the interchange. Last thing he needed was a boat of pirates thinking this girl was a treasure to be conquered and shared. She winced at his grip but he had no time for niceties. His body craved attention and his mind demanded he maintain control of this ship, this crew, as they came closer to the prize he wanted.

Reeling her into his cabin, he kicked the door shut. "For a lady, you appear to have run from all the rules of society. Stowaway on a pirate ship, unable to follow the simplest of instructions, and helping yourself to another's clothing, which I do believe is called stealing." He seethed with each word but managed to quirk a tight grin at the end.

The fear in her eyes disappeared. "How dare you accuse me of being either stowaway or thief! As to your orders, I did remain here but that would have left me to starvation!" She stood, shoulders back, tense. Her face flush with a glowing red. And that damn crumb that didn't budge. The hunger for her grew.

Then, her tongue slipped out, stole the bread from her luscious lips and darted back inside. His breath skipped.

"As to borrowing your clothes…"

His brows inched higher. Borrowing. He'd never wash them again, a voice deep inside him snickered. His cock twitched.

"It was deemed better to keep my tattered gown on, a dress destroyed by my escape, on a ship full of men?"

"Escape? Your memory returns?"

She shook her head. "No. I have images, very short, and a feeling of being chased. That must be how I ended up on your ship, not to sail away with pirates, but to escape."

Unfortunately, it was a wrong choice to fall onto this vessel. They were at sea, nothing more could be done for the moment. He started to pace.

"It may bring more awareness to you if we return you to the docks. Perhaps your family will be looking for you." He paused and looked at her. "Or your husband?" Though a quick glimpse at her hand showed no signs of a wedding band or even an indentation one had been there. He battered the quick excitement that raced through him of her being free of marriage. What the hell was he thinking?

The blood drained from her face turning it ghastly white with fear and those stunning blue eyes widened again.

"No! Please! Do not take me back there!"

Chapter Seven

JAMES RACED THROUGH THE WHARF, searching for any evidence of Eleanor. He had not thought Dryer's was a name hard to find but neither had he frequented the waterfront and its many stores and warehouses. Of course, what if it was a ship's name? He scanned the horizon hours ago and was greeted by a multitude of ships. It was too much.

Clearwater caught up to him as they topped another slope of wooden walkways.

"I dare say, ole chap, wherever might they've taken her?"

"If I knew that, I'd have her back in my arms." He swallowed his frustration and adjusted his waistcoat. The skies were clearing and once more, the air was thick with moisture and rising heat.

Clearwater skidded on the damp wooden walkway. "I really had no notion the dangers of being here. No wonder proper gentlemen do not linger in the shipyards."

James snorted. "No, it lacks your quality of prime entertainment. No boxing house, fencing yards, mews or ladies anywhere here I've seen. Lowly gin joints, women of loose quality and sailors and dockworkers that could pound a fist readily into any likely gent, though abound."

"Since we are speaking of better amusements…"

James shook his head, still walking and scanning for names on buildings. "We are not."

Clearwater ignored his words but continued plowing after him. "Perhaps a minor break would refresh you, and me, of course."

In that split second, James stopped and turned, halting his friend.

"I know she is not your wife, nor is she a concern to you in any fashion, outside being my wife. While I do appreciate your aid, I would understand if you chose to find other entertainment."

Clearwater's mouth dropped open in shock. "James, I have been your friend throughout our entire lives. You need help and while you have servants spread far searching, what type of friend would I be to abandon you now?" He slapped James's arm. "Besides, what better way to get a kiss from the lady and be touted a hero in aiding you finding her? Harrumph!"

With that, James couldn't help but chuckle. "Now, that sounds like you. Come, we've turned this section dry. Onto the next."

They marched another set walkways before they came upon two surly men nailing boards over hole in the wall, their grumblings along with their audible spitting was too much to be missed. And above the doorway, on the side, was a sign that read Dryer's Imports. James took off toward the ruins.

"Say here," he said, sliding to a stop on the wet boards. "We were hoping you might aid us."

The two workers glared at them, one with spit at the corner of his mouth. Both looked like ragged dock workers and not happy with the current job. Neither one spoke. Ill-mannered brutes.

"I'm looking for…" he began, but Clearwater interrupted him.

"Hate to bother you chaps but we can make it worth your while." He nudged James.

"Ah, yes." James reached into his waistcoat and withdrew a couple of shillings. "Perhaps this will amend for you taking a break from your current endeavors."

The older one didn't wait and snagged the coins. "Whatcha be wantin', gov'na?"

"I'm looking for a lady, one who is fair of skin and brown hair. One perhaps drawn here by others…" he paused, eying them and deciding they were exactly the type he was thinking of. "…of ill-will. Have you seen such a lady?"

The man toyed with the coins, his lips drawn tight. The other one jabbed him.

"Yes sir, we done seen a chit like that," the smaller man answered. "In fac', she was the one who made this damn hole—"

"Yes, we've seen the type," the first man interrupted. "Must've been holed up here, from the looks of it. Heard she escaped."

James lost all patience as rage exploded. These men took his wife and he would have answers! He grabbed the man by his arms and jerked him upright, the shillings falling through the planks to splash in the water below.

"Oh, I bet you do know all about her," he seethed. "And whoever put you up to this, for surely as nitwitted as you are, to seal a hole of your escapee isn't likely but ordered to by your benefactor? Yes." He slammed the man up against the remains of the building wall. "Where did she run to?"

The man tried to squirm free but James held him tight.

"We ain't sure. Please, my lord, we done her no harm!"

"You took her from me by force! Do not take me as a mouse! I will take in return what was stolen from me! Now, where the hell is she?"

∞

A WAVE OF NAUSEAM WASHED OVER her at the mere hint of returning to the docks. She swallowed the bile that reached the back of her throat as she clutched her hands into small fists, trying to stop the tremors that threatened. Visions, faint like ghosts, flittered through her thoughts. She needed these demons to go away but instead, they taunted her, claiming they'd get her. Anger threatened to overtake her. She would not go back and that was all there was about it!

The captain frowned, obviously not understanding her fear. But then, this was a man who fired cannonballs at other ships and stole their goods. She should be wary of him. But there was something about him that also made her want to melt. High cheekbones and a square jawline, Trent Cavendish was a fascination for her. A faint voice in the back of her head wondered how he'd look in a frock coat and breeches the stylish men of the ton wore. The musing hitched her thoughts. How did she know that? Of course, the remains of her own gown did give her the impression of good breeding.

The silence between them became thick as the wool frock she imagined him in. But her mouth was too dry to speak, her mind bombarded with wicked thoughts and of fears from ghostly images. She bit her lower lip.

Trent's brows furrowed as he leaned back against his desk.

"I did not mean to startle you. I had thought returning you would make you happy, perhaps trigger more memories, not nightmares." He shook his head and pushed off the side of the desktop. "Darlin', see here..." he paused. "I don't expect a name has popped into that pretty little head of yours?"

Another problem. She struggled through the web of her thoughts when she heard a voice, deep, fighting to be heard. "El...El..."

"El? Rather odd. Elle, perhaps? Elizabeth?"

Neither of those sounded right but she was too exhausted trying to clear the mess of her mind to care. She shot him a sad shrug, not caring at this minute what he called her.

He laughed. The ringing tone soothed her ears. It was deep and seductive. Oh bother...

"We shall use Elle. It rolls off the tongue easily, that is if you will." He cocked his head. "Or shall we try Elizabeth?" He gave her a dazzling smile.

She was mesmerized by him. He was danger and temptation, a puzzle that stirred a fire deep inside her. She swallowed hard. There were bigger issues to work with and her allure to him was not one.

"Elle will be fine." There was a certain way it sounded that made her wonder if it was her name.

But all thoughts of pushing him aside fell to ruin as he took a step closer to her, still with that devil-may-care grin, and reached for a tendril that fell, touching her shoulder. Her heart skipped a beat but she couldn't drag her eyes off him.

He was grinning but that smile wasn't reflected in his gaze. What she saw was a whirling stream of emotion ranging from seduction to curiosity to bitterness. What was he thinking?

A pounding at the door interrupted them right as the door swung wide.

"Capt'n, think you'll wanna take a gander at this." Fitzgibbons stormed in, ignoring them and plopping a ledger book, opened, on the desktop.

Instantly, the captain's eyes hardened as he spun to see the book. Elle stepped back, her heart still beating fast, her blood still on fire from him. Something hinted in the back of her cluttered head it was for the best this happened. He was too close, the desire that pooled inside her too ignited, to expect to be ignored. He would have kissed her, she was sure of that. She had to dampen this burning desire for him because he was danger.

∞

TRENT WANTED TO BEAT FITZGIBBONS and to thank him all in the same breath. Inside, his blood raced, his loins burned to be buried inside her and what was left of his rational mind told him to run. The first mate answered his question over what he should do. He was to refocus and find the person who got Rachel killed.

He blinked, trying to erase the thought of Elle's lips, her petite luscious body all within his arms' reach. Forcing himself to concentrate, he focused on the page the first mate pointed to. The lines held the scrawl of the captain Trent had questioned just a short while ago. That man claimed to know nothing but his log indicated he was a liar.

Dated six months ago was the manifest of the *Prestige* and on it was Rachel Cavendish. As he scanned the next two pages, white hot anger poured through his veins, his vision red as the captain reported a "mishap" at sea involving a ship with black sails and the name Matilda. He hissed.

"So, the ghost rises."

Fitzgibbons nodded. "Ain't it amazin' how a ship, so lost

at sea, weighted too much ta sail after the storm and it sank, managed ta find sail again."

"We all know what happened. Damn Spanish can't admit they too fall prey, thinkin' their wickedness out-weighs pirate luck." He slammed the book shut. "Worst is, I let that son of bitch go when I should have hung him from the yardarm for hiding this from me!" He shoved his hand into his hair while he paced what little he could in a cabin that was now crowded.

"Did ya notice the post of where the capt'n thought the ship was headed?"

"He made mention of it turning west with it's new cargo in place along with new recruits who went on the account." The account being they turned pirate. A lucra-tive position that paid higher than any sailor got though the price tag was high—death by hanging, the sentence for all pirates. He knew well as he, too, had gone on the account months ago. With his mind calculating, reached for the rum bottle sitting on top of the shelf over the desk.

"Did ya notice the markin' in the front of the log, men-tioning the home port of the ship? And how home ain't listed?" Fitzgibbons took the offered cup and raised it in unspoken celebration.

Trent raised his as his lips curved in satisfaction. "Yes, and to it's port we shall go."

The cups clashed as the men roared a festive sound. As he took a swig of the rum, Trent realized Elle stood in the corner, her head tilted in a questioning look. He'd forgotten the woman. And only minutes ago, he's battled with his will to throw on his bed, making mad passionate love, or throw her into the waves. He now berated his lack of manners. The news took him back to his driving force and disrupted any desires he held in either direction in regard to her. In a quick motion, he poured her a drink and offered it.

"Good news, a thing I've been looking for." He raised his cup and she mimicked his move.

"Hear, hear," she said softly, and raised the cup to her lips.

A jolt of desire stabbed him deep when she sipped and he saw her throat working to drink the dark brew. His cock thickened again and he diverted his gaze in hopes of stopping the wicked member from hardening, which would be highly visible pressed against his trousers. If nothing else, he needed to re-think his course. Elle or Matilda and a price due. He peered at her above the rim of his cup as he swallowed the end of the rum. Desire for her could steer him from his goal, one that now lay so close to grab. That and the twitch in his groin snapped him to attention. He had a crew to appease to get them to take the course he needed. But first, to off load a prize he did not take and couldn't keep.

Fitzgibbons coughed to grab his attention. He grinned. The Irishman was well talented in making him veer back on track. Without taking his gaze off the woman, he ordered, "Have us head west, Fitzgibbons."

"Aye, aye, Capt'n."

The girl cocked her head to the right, a questioning look on her face. It caused a nerve to crackle, for she would not like his conclusion. But he tired of battle and needed sleep.

"Get some rest. Perhaps that'll make your mind right itself. We'll discuss your plans later." As he turned to the cabin door, he made his escape before she asked him more because he couldn't tell her their first stop was London.

Chapter Eight

"THEY WERE SNIVELING BASTARDS, NOTH-ING more." Clearwater downed the contents of his glass and sighed. "But now, after two bloody weeks hunting, you've got a name to go by. All well and good." He smiled broadly as he slouched back in stuffed chair at Brooks.

James stared at his glass of brandy, the liquor barely touched. Two weeks without his Eleanor felt more like a lifetime. He coughed, clearing his mind of that fact and returned to now. "They were commoners of the lowest quality. Spilling the name of some ship no longer in port told us nothing. For all I know, the ship wasn't real—"

"Posh!" Clearwater spitted out. "You did check with the harbor master and found a ship by that name in the ledger."

Finally taking a sip, James relished the burn that scorched his throat and fired his belly. At this point, the pain was the only thing that made him feel alive.

"Yes, a ship with that name *Equuleus* was there but no longer. And you heard the rumors."

"Pirate/privateer, all one and the same in time of war."

But with his wife taken as hostage? Narrowed the field down to simply pirate. Fear raed down his spine. "We wasted valuable time downing drink while she…"

Clearwater moved to the edge of his seat. "It is night, James. Now is not the time to sail, looking for a ship that could fit into the docks, a pirate ship, and not go noticed. Do you think you'd find her at night, under the glow of the stars and moon?"

Damn! He didn't want to admit his friend was right. With a deep sigh, he sat back, sitting the snifter down on the table nearby. Contemplating his next step, he eyed Clearwater.

"While I appreciate your help in my search, do you not a one of your own? For the future Lady Clearwater?"

Clearwater snorted. "I have met and pursued such a miss only to have my affections tossed to the side while another stole her heart." He gave James a half smile. "And her dowry. I, of course, was the better match, but her father deemed the other superior." He shrugged.

James frowned at his friend. "And who was this lady of valor? Where was I, to have missed this tragedy?"

Clearwater snagged James's glass and downed the entire contents. "You, my friend, had your bollocks tied to knots seeking Lady Eleanor's hand, too busy to waste time of the world around you." At his move to protest, Clearwater's waved him down. "There is no reason to apologize, my friend. In the game of marriage, one must work to find a wife, not worry if dearest friend marries or not."

James caught the flicker in Lord Clearwater's eyes, a flash that did not look like love or even lust when he mentioned the lady. No, there was a quick look of anger before Clearwater's easy smile returned. It made him wonder what had happened. Before he could inquire, his friend stood.

"From what you discovered today from those miscreants, you have your work cut out for you tomorrow. Think sleep should be your top priority."

James smiled, following Clearwater to the front of the club where they retrieved their hats and frocks before finding their horses. As the horses clip-clopped down the street toward James's townhouse, Clearwater slowed near his own place but before he dismounted, James reached over and grabbed his arm.

"I would appreciate any further time you have to help me on the morrow."

Clearwater snorted. "I wouldn't miss this adventure for anything in the world. Good night."

"Good night," James replied as Clearwater bounded the stairs to his residence and snuck inside .

The trip to the townhouse was short but long enough for him to feel the exhaustion of all the time spent searching catch up to him. In fact, he almost tripped up the stairs to the door and laughed, since he acted as if drunk without even finishing one drink. The butler at the door was not amused. Trent ignored the stern-faced servant, leaving his coat, hat and gloves with him and turned toward the stairs, leaping up them quickly.

The townhouse had been his favorite bachelor residence, always within short distant to the club, the social center of London and the gambling halls where youthful single lords hung, spending family money with ardor. And the ladies....not proper but the improper ones that hugged on him, had offered enjoyment beyond measure. That was until he met Eleanor, then his world changed.

The fireplace in his room glowed with the embers of a low fire. He sighed. His help was exceptional, and must have spies out to find when he would be in residence.

The welcoming glow from the burning fire seeped into his bones and he'd gladly wanted to give in but not now. Quickly, he tore off his waistcoat and kicked his shoes to the side, stretching. Sleep. He hoped it would come for it had eluded him before. With that doubt in his mind, he strode to the table in the corner of his room and poured himself a shot of rum that had come in the last shipment of goods from his lands in the West Indies. The rum had a settling, if not burning, effect on him.

He did not wait for the butler to come help him change for bed. No, Trent would do it himself. Shoving his breeches to the floor, he grabbed his drink and walked to his bed, eager to jump in and fall asleep. He reached for the curtain that fell around the head of the bed and came to a sudden, complete stop.

Sitting in the center of his bed, dressed in a blue lace dressing gown, was someone that totally surprised him. The dove white-skinned goddess with the tangle of dark curls brushing her shoulders was obviously there to attract him. But still, it stunned him.

"Lydia. What a surprise to see you here."

She smiled.

He was doomed.

∞

THE SEA HAD ALWAYS BEEN a balm to soothe his soul. Always. So why was he now so conflicted?

Trent stood on the upper deck, scanning the map in his hands, listening to reports from Fitzgibbons about the ship and their course, but when she walked onto the deck, his senses picked up and the turmoil inside him started again. He couldn't even take his eyes off her, despite his desperate attempts to do so. At least she no longer wore his clothes, well, not his pants. He had found a smaller pair in the hold, left by a sailor sometime ago, a man who stood shorter than the rest of the men. The shirt, though, he couldn't, no, wouldn't replace. There was something vastly appealing to his inner soul for her to wear what was his. As if she was his... He cursed inwardly at that thought. No one would ever replace Rachel.

Yet, even now, this woman appeared to float across the planks in the early morning light. Dawn at sea was always a glorious event and she added to it, as if she were an angel.

"And with that, the cow moved into the cottage..."

Trent heard that remark and knew Fitzgibbons was rattling him. "I heard that."

"Didcha now? Could've sworn if I said the pope was next to ya, you'd agree," the Irishman grumbled. "Why not bed the wench and get her out of your blood?"

"You know I won't do that." Anger took control, yet was the man far off the mark? In memory of his wife, Trent hoped not.

"You're a stubborn boy, Capt'n, stubborn." Fitzgibbons shook his head. "It'll be your undoin'."

Trent inhaled deeply and physically turned away from the overview of his ship's decking in a way to block his vision of her. "Repeat what you were saying, minus the cow."

"Jus' that your course to the West Indies, while all well and good, with a stop in London and its nest of naval ships and waitin' nooses if we're seen, has got the men stirrin'."

Trent grinded his teeth. His attempt to rid himself of the siren below did put them in serious trouble. The *Prestige*, if discovered, would add to his reputation as pirate and all his men too. The Crown had given a blind eye for most of the war against France to any privateer whose sights might veer off simply French targets, except when it meant English. He'd crossed that line perhaps once too often.

"So, if given word, what do you recommend, outside of carnal desires." There was no point in denying attraction to the girl. But not acting on it was what he needed to do. Steeling his guts, he forced himself to focus on now.

"The watch has caught sight of a ship, nigh off the coastline due south, bearing the markings of The *Raptor*."

That did indeed catch his attention. "In these waters?"

"Aye."

The ship was a pirate ship, one that he saw listed in the book off the *Prestige*. "Makes one wonder what they're searching for. No riches lay here, outside a bounty of naval ships and those protected by the crown."

"Aye, but there are those like the *Prestige* that are likely full of prizes."

"Not enough to lure a ship of those colors. She normally lurks closer south. Yet it does make one wonder what she might be holding."

Fitzgibbons laughed. "It is a way to protect ourselves, to make her appear that she went afta our stop and not us."

Tapping the tabletop absently, Trent's mind worked fast. To attack another pirate ship was bad form in this world of black sails, but to be able to glean more information might work.

"All right, then veer south by southwest, Mr. Fitzgibbons, and let us find what we can."

"Aye, aye, Capt'n!"

As the Irishman went marched off, issuing the orders to change course, Trent found his passenger. She stood near the gunwale, hands on the railing, staring out on the sea. He needed to release her from his ship, calm his men's fears and re-direct them to his orders as they headed west. A tiny voice deep within him clamored to be heard, not to let her go nor trust the other ship to return her.

But to keep her here would be the death of him. That he was sure. His cock twitched reminding him so. Revenge and seduction made lousy bedmates. Hell!

Chapter Nine

ELLE HEARD THE COMMANDS BEING shouted across the deck and the scurrying of bare feet as the pirates jumped to life, quickly dropping their chores to manning the rigging, turning the direction of the sails that billowed under the sea's wind thus changing the direction of the ship. She found nothing on the new horizon that she could see to spur such excitement. Frankly, she'd been lost in her own thoughts, trying to organize the visions that plopped into her mind and vanished before she could grasp them. These had images of her past trying to break through the maze in her muddled thoughts and when she thought she had one, the throbbing in her temple made her wince and abandon the pursuit. The ship's surgeon had told her to relax and her memory would return when her injuries healed, she just had no idea part of those injuries included her mind.

Being outside, facing the sea and inhaling the fresh salt air soothed her and she found herself here probably more than Cavendish wanted. She tried to make herself not a nuisance and out of the reach of the pirates but often caught a glimpse of them eyeing her. He, himself, was often among them, but his gaze was heated, igniting fires in areas he shouldn't be able to. Her nipples tingled, her nerves twitched, and the core of her was like lava.

At times, the want for him drove her mad.

Last night, as the sun set, he brought her dinner. He set it on the table without a word to her and left the cabin, slamming the door behind him. All his actions pointed to the fact he was furious, as if she'd done something wrong. It infuriated her for she did not mean to end up on this ship. She had no idea it was a pirate ship nor that it was leaving the docks, all she knew was it was an avenue to escape those monsters chasing her and she took it without a second thought. That memory was perfectly clear to her, for those creatures still pursued her whenever she closed her eyes.

The captain never returned last night, or not that she could tell. She ate little, her stomach flipping at the mere idea that she was in his cabin, though from what she gathered, Cavendish was in the only cabin. The rest of the crew shared the rest—not the ideal situation for her at all. A shiver went down her spine with the thought that since she was with him and how the rest were out, the indication was clear. She was the captain's woman and under his protection. Somehow that meant more than what happened here, between them. Her thoughts mangled with the idea and the confusion that still flooded her mind. Sleep. She needed sleep. So she grabbed the woolen blanket off the cot, wrapped herself in it and curled at the foot of the bed, trying to sleep. But anytime she started to dream, the nightmare of her past sprung ghosts that scared her awake.

Now, as the ship swung on the waves in a new direction, her nerves bolted. Was he attacking another ship she couldn't yet see? Or was he taking them far away and she'd never be free? Her head hurt from the dilemma, for she could not see a way for her at all here or on land. Her breathing stuttered and her heart pounded hard. So hard that it made breathing almost impossible. What was she to do?

Refocusing on the water to calm her fraying nerves, she didn't hear him approach and jumped when he spoke.

"I need you to return to the cabin, my dear."

"You planning another raid?" The words spilled from her mouth fast before she realized it.

He snorted, giving her a lopsided grin. It was a cocky smile that took her breath away. "Perhaps. And if that's the circumstance, I fear for your safety. You'd be considered a prize, as the case may be." He shrugged.

Now she was confused. "You fancy me a trophy?"

"You are pretty enough to say yes. And on the seas, in a world of men, a lady of your stature is like Helen of Troy—enough beauty for men to fight for. So I beg for your future and for that of my ship, you retire to my cabin."

"A cabin you abandon for me?" Why was she testing him? Not even she could figure that out except the fire inside her ignited. She wanted him to kiss her.

"For your safety, again, it is better to be there than any-where else. My men will leave you be if you are under my care. Without it, you would see the darker side of man, one ruled by carnal pleasures of the type you would not wish for."

She swallowed. She'd seen the other pirates, some of which were filthy, some had broken teeth, scars and a stench that if it weren't for the open air, she'd retch. She nodded but wasn't happy. The stuffiness of the room would drive her mad.

He offered her his arm. It was a gentlemanly gesture, one that seemed out of place on a pirate ship. But manners she'd been trained dictated her place her hand on it. The whole notion sent a thrill through her, not only of his offering but also the electricity that shot through her as she touched him.

He took her to the cabin. Neither of them said a word. Her gaze was fixed on his. Those gorgeous brown eyes of his, the color of chocolate, seemed heated. She'd give anything to know if he, too, felt the tingle that raced through her.

Once inside, he closed the door with a kick and spun her into his embrace. With a boldness that shocked her, he wrapped his arms around her middle, pulling her tight against him. Her breasts smashed against him, his muscled thighs against hers. She couldn't breathe, but this time, her racing heart wasn't frantic with fear but with desire.

Still speechless, he bent and his lips claimed hers. His kiss was tame until his tongue darted out, licking against her mouth, begging for entrance. She lost her fear and parted her lips. He growled as his tongue invaded her. It was a kiss that was deep, inviting, dangerously hot and needy. It matched her own and she relished in it.

And as suddenly as he started it, he broke off, setting her back a step. His gaze burned and his chest heaved. Still silent, he turned on his heel and virtually fled from the room.

She gulped for air. Emotions mixed deep inside her. He shouldn't have kissed her. She wanted him to but didn't. And from appearances, it seemed that this strong pirate captain must have had thoughts equal to hers, with how quickly he hastened his departure.

What was she going to do? Why did she feel like she just sinned? And why did she want more?

෴

"LYDIA, THIS IS AN UNEXPECTED surprise." A very unwanted surprise. James shouldn't have been that unaware. The woman wasn't pleased to have their relationship ended but when he married Eleanor, all dalliances came to a halt. The last time he saw Lydia, she had stormed out, furious at him.

"She'll never love you like I do, James Haddington. Never!"

The words echoed down the hallway as her heels clipped on the wood floors. All his servants disappeared as they moved out of her path.

Now that Eleanor was gone, Lydia returned. He shook his head.

She smiled at him in a coquette's way. "I came to give comfort and ease your pain at your loss."

"I haven't lost anything, Lydia."

Her smile broadened and she shifted, her shoulders straightened, as if she was the queen. "Viscount of Clearwater states otherwise. And I know you, hiding your pain. I just wanted to make you smile."

Lydia St. Martin, the third daughter of the aging Viscount Attlewood, simply was a girl easily left by her family with too much freedom. Being the middle daughter, her ability to blend in left her too much liberties to mischief. He'd met her at a soiree two years ago, one that had quickly dissolved into a party of too much liquor and closed doors. The type very few available ladies had attended and most of them were absent when the bubbly increased and the clothes decreased. She stood to the side, as if a statue, watching. And he, himself, too many drinks to be held accountable, struck up conversation with her.

The rest, he cared to forget. She was pretty, her long

dark hair soft, her dark eyes inviting, and her body way too available for him to ignore. They were lovers, one he hadn't regretted at the time. After all, she wasn't a virgin and promised to a shipping heir of the gentry elite, an overweight vermin by all accounts. So when he informed her their relationship was over, James was greeted with an onslaught of emotions from her— disbelief, tears, and finally anger. How could he think to end it with her? They'd both be able to continue, despite their marital status. And how could he throw her love away?

"Just how did you gain entrance?" He inched his eyebrows up, indicating he meant entrance to more than just the house.

She smiled and slid from the bed. Thankfully, her dressing gown covered her well, though it didn't hide how her nipples had hardened. He gritted his teeth, his shoulders locked and he fisted his hands. Lydia was way too seductive and she knew it. She took a step closer to him. He refused to move when her right hand raised to his face, her fingers smoothing his forehead.

"Worry lines do not become you." The softly spoken remark tried to touch a sympathy cord to him, and failed.

He spun and stepped toward the sideboard, pouring himself a brandy. "Where is your husband, my dear? Mr. Wattsmore too detained to notice your absence?"

Her lips curled in disdain. "No, actually he's aboard his ship, matters of importance, or so he uttered, in the colonies. He sailed for the West Indies last week."

He could hear the fabric of her gown, a gossamer piece, filmy and voluminous, rustle behind him.

"He is practicing to be a woeful husband. I need a man to fill his lack of priority," she whispered, a mew at the end.

He downed the liquor in one swallow, battling memories

of her body that her close stance, almost pressing against him, came crashing in. She was a delectable woman, but despite the base desires he had held for her once, Lydia was not Eleanor and could never reach the love he held for his wife—a grip so strong it was like a buoy during a violent sea tempest.

"My dear, what you need is to remember your marriage vows and how you swore you'd love, honor and obey your husband—"

"Him? Eugene is not a member of the ton, nor will he ever gain that position." She huffed in disgust and paced the floor. James silently prayed thanks for the separation. "Besides," she continued. "How can it be dishonor when he is not of our class? It most definitely allows me—"

"Lydia, it is beneath you, you as a lady, to be here." He eyed her carefully. The lover he had known had turned bitter in her marriage. That could be dangerous.

She stopped and looked at him. "It is considered virtually a given for noblemen to have their courtesans or mistresses, to frequent the whoring houses. In fact, sympathy reigns high if his is a forced marriage or one so poorly mated. But for me? I'm simply to stay at the house and be solitary?"

It was true. For ladies, there was no recourse to take against a husband's infidelity. A loveless marriage marred many households. "Unfortunately, yes. You are meant to enhance your husband's position and maintain the look of a proper lady. Crawling into another man's bed? No."

Lydia stood quietly. The flowing dressing gown would give her the angelic appearance she longed for but the quiver in her lip drew the adoration away. If she turned to tears, he'd be doomed because he couldn't kick her out in that state. Biting back his frustration, he went to her, gripping her upper arms, wondering if he should shake understanding into her head. Probably doubtful, so he simply held her steady as her eyes watered.

But before a single tear spilled, she swallowed hard and the smile returned. It was a grin that did not reach her eyes. Squaring her shoulders, she shook his hands away.

"You should not be angry with me. Albert only told me you were getting frantic, irritable and irrational. He muttered a distraction might take the worry off your shoulders, so you could think more clearly." She shrugged, but the smile remained.

Of course, she figured a quick twirl in the sheets would distract him. With her? The distraction would not turn out like she wanted. If nothing else, if she'd climbed into his bed without his knowledge, the results would be devastating.

"Go home, Lydia. Have a child or three. Let that be your distraction and a way to prevent your appearance in this room again."

Her grin turned lopsided as she reached for her clothes off the side chair. "I won't plead for you to reconsider nor to leave this room so I can change. But I will tell you this, if your wife perishes during this separation, the vultures will not bat an eye at my presence and you may need it to help you recover from your loss. And then, you'll regret admonishing me so easily."

Within two steps, she was before him. She stood on her toes and gave him peck on his lips before she grabbed her clothes and shoes and left.

Chapter Ten

SITTING ON THE BANNISTER, HER back to the railing, she let her feet dangle. It was strange to feel the planking under her soles. In the early morning, the warming boards were soothing, but by late afternoon, the surface burned. The pain probably was more keenly felt by her than the others as they had callused feet. But her heels, toes, and soles were soft to the touch, nary a callus in sight. Apparently "ladies" always wore slippers and if they were anything like the pair she had, well, no physical labor would ever get done. Why would a lady do so if it meant destroying her shoes?

She also had to get comfortable in trousers—something she had never worn, that she was sure of. But the twill was course and rubbed on her inner thighs, causing a rash. And her blouse, or shirt, was cotton, not the soft material like her tattered gown. The fabric didn't touch her skin as much as she still wore her corset. To go without, that was downright uncomfortable and allowed that fabric to scrape against her smooth, soft body. She sighed. She'd adjust because she had no choice.

The sun poured down from the heavens, glistening off the ocean around them. She shoved the battered hat further down her head to give her shade plus it held the bulk of her hair, all wound up loosely, off her neck. She bit back a groan. What she wouldn't give for a fan.

"You be bakin' out here, missy."

She glanced up with a grin spreading across her face. Fitzgibbons. The Irishman met her with a cherubic smile of his own. He had been the only one truly kind to her. Standing a good head taller than her, even a touch taller than the captain, his rusty hair was sprinkled in grey, his face and hands were leathery from the sun exposure. Dark brown eyes held amusement even now as he glanced down at her.

"I'll be fine." She scooted for him to sit next to her but he didn't. "I must again thank you for the hat. It's done wonders."

He chuckled. "Just an old thing rummaging around. Plus it helps block the sun from your pretty face. Though, I suspect you're feelin' a touch heated."

She laughed. "I do believe you're correct." With a quick glance at hands and feet, she peered up at him. "And I think I'm a bit pinked from the sun."

"Aye, lassie, that you are." He reached into the bag he had and pulled a jar from it. "An ointment, secured from Doc, tha' make the burn ease."

She took the jar and pulled the large round cork top out. The substance was yellowish and creamy, like a pudding. Puzzled, she took a sniff and a fragrant aroma filled her nostrils. "Honey?"

"Aye, a wee ole concoction, from one of the isles." He leaned forward, his voice lowering. "It also helps wee parched lips as well." He winked.

"Sir, I do believe you be flattering me."

He shot her a look of surprise but she knew he wasn't.

"Oh, really? Is tha' such a bad thing?"

She reached out and touched his hand. "No, it isn't. I thank you. Your presence makes me feel a little safer."

"Och, what hav' ye to fear here?"

She swallowed. "The captain for one. He makes it plainly clear I am nothing more than a trifle, an inconvenience that he'd just assume rid himself of."

"Oh, lass, don't worry about the boy, uh, the captain, so badly. He's faced hard times, with his woman taken against her will and nothin' could be done." He shrugged, his gaze full of sympathy.

"She was taken? Is she still missing?" That'd explain the man's anger toward her. She had escaped her situation, which the vague hints in her mind told her wasn't necessarily good. But the captain had a wife? And someone took her?

Fitzgibbons shifted, his head tilted toward the upper deck. "Ach, he found the lass. Dead by the hands of man too crafty ta be caught."

Elle bit her bottom lip, her brow creased as she thought about this. "What a sad story. Is that what drove him to piracy? Or was he already pirate? If so, is that what brought this? Revenge for a raid? And if that is the case, what did she think of his life as a thief?"

The Irishman chuckled, his bronzed cheeks turning ruddy red. "Capt'n is right. You do ask many a question."

She said nothing, only shot him a questioning gaze. Again, he looked at the upper deck, where she saw the captain. Made her wonder if the man was sent to check about her, or more likely, see if she'd regained her memory. She doubted it was truly to share secrets about the handsome rogue who ruled the ship. If nothing else, she couldn't help be become more intrigued by him. She smiled at the first mate.

SENDING FITZGIBBONS TO TALK TO her was a mistake.

Trent's jaw tightened. He stood on the upper deck, ostensibly, to check the maps and plot the ship's course. Instead, he found his attention drifted to the lower deck and the girl who had no memory. The one who took over his cabin. The one who stole into his thoughts—and worse. He sighed and redirected his gaze on the ocean before his ship. He should take her back to London, drop her at the docks, or perhaps at Madame's house. He instantly scratched that thought. A whorehouse for a lady of her beauty would be bad, especially with no memory, for Madame Beauvoir was always on the lookout for new girls. Anyone else, he could not consider as his reputation had sullied since he last donned the clothes of a gentleman.

The waves called to him and, once more, he concentrated on the sea, listening to her sounds, finding that rhythm subdued frayed, overwrought nerves. The sea life had adopted him, filling his veins with a freedom he'd never find on English lands. A giggle drifted to his ears.

The Irishman got her to laugh? Damn the man. Despite his best attempt to lose himself in the sea, the siren down below drew him back. He uttered another curse under his breath when he found her sitting where she was, dressed simply in the course trousers and linen shirt that billowed in the breeze. The straw hat covered her head and with her hair wound up under the crown, gave the appearance of a young lad, especially since the brim covered much of her face. But it didn't hide her mouth—that luscious set of lips that beckoned to him. Her glowing smile set off an anger deep inside him. An anger at himself for even taking notice. The fact that the smile sent a bolt of desire made him want to drop her anywhere for fear he'd drive himself into her if he didn't.

He had sent the first mate down with the jar of ointment when he couldn't help but notice her skin turning from pink to red from the sun. What he didn't expect was her opening it and dipping her fingers in. His body tightened. She withdrew them, the medicine dripped from her fingers and his groin twitched. Something Fitzgibbons said made her pause, give him a quick smile and turn back to applying the medicine. She perched her right foot heel on the railing, which exposed her ankle and shapely calf. The act made his mouth go dry. Nothing she did resembled the manly appearance her clothes depicted. Even the simply act of lifting her foot showed her upbringing—her dainty foot raised slowly, deliberately, up to the railing. She nodded to something Fitzgibbons was saying. Then she applied the ointment to the top of her barefoot and his heart skipped a beat as his cock hardened.

Son of a gun! This was torture!

When the Irishman laughed with her, Trent thought he'd lose his mind. He jumped, trying to control his body's reaction to her. Every second he watched only convinced him she was a lady, with ladylike manners, her body movements flowed like the water they floated on. Without thinking, he smacked the telescope down, and fled down the stairs to the lower deck and found himself standing near her before he realized in his thinking, his gaze fixated on her small, dainty foot. As he watched, her toes curled under, nearly pushing him to madness, claiming her here and now.

"Capt'n, the lady and I were discussin'—"

"Yes, I see. Quite the conversationalist you are, matey. I

believe your mission was a simple task. To deliver to her a salve for the burn, not prolong her presence out in this baking sun," he hissed.

Fitzgibbons was stunned, but not for long. "Laddie, let's not travel down the path you be on."

She glared at him. Her sparkling sapphire gaze zeroing in on him. "Captain Cavendish, let me reassure you, you are very much out of line here!"

God, she was beautiful. When she stood, the hat shifted and a curled lock fell upon her shoulder. It dangled and drove the lust in his veins hotter.

"You shouldn't be out here. It is driving the men crazy," he snarled. He'd seen his men ogling her for way too long. And it wasn't only them. The woman was driving him to distraction—an emotion he hadn't felt since Rachel.

She gasped. "And where would you expect me to be? In your cabin all day long?" The questions rose in volume as she braced herself, as if he'd attack her. He might, if given the chance... He stopped the thought, shocked at where his train of thought went.

So he met her challenge with his best lopsided smile, or the one most women, especially his wife, said ranked him a true rogue. "Perhaps you'd like to find out how cabins can be a safe place."

Her reaction was immediate. "I beg your pardon?"

He took a step closer. With a lower voice, he added, "Wonder what that might involve?"

Her eyes widened and her mouth dropped open but the shock passed and her lips closed to a single, tight line. She hissed and stormed past him, toward the cabin. The next noise was the door slamming, the sound reverberated throughout the ship.

Trent laughed.

"Do you know wha' you're doin' lad?" The Irishman's

question held a warning tone.

This time his smile was genuine. "Aye, first time in a long time, I do." He laughed and went back to his perch with his maps and looking glass, silently pleased.

Once back on the upper deck, he stared at the maps, moving a knife that weighted the parchment drawings to the table as the sea breeze raced by, still grinning. But the joy evaporated when it hit him she was adorable, flustered and nettled in her worn outfit made for a man. The oversized trousers and shirt only accentuated her petite form. It made him want to curse.

"Tell me, boy, what you were thinkin', testing her so."

Fitzgibbons. He sent the man to keep an eye on her since after that kiss, he didn't trust himself with her. In fact, it was that kiss that still haunted his waking thoughts. So did the anger that wrapped itself around the memory. He snapped the looking glass open and forced himself to scan the horizon.

It was time to answer the first mate. "Just trying to provoke a memory of her past. That is all."

"By seducing her?"

He laughed hollowly. "Bedding her is not my objective." He shuffled the maps on the table. But he realized Fitzgibbons wasn't moving at all. "Is there something else?"

"Well, Capt'n, perhaps you should. It could be wha' ya be needin'. Perhaps wha' she needs, too."

"To bed her?" Even the thought made his stomach tighten. A vision of her naked flickered through his mind, one he instantly squashed.

"It'd be far better than sleepin' here." He leaned on the table. "It's sendin' a message to the lads that maybe she free, maybe even be wantin' a man."

"Nah…"

Fitzgibbons's eyebrows raised, questioning him. Trent

grunted. Something about this woman ate at his gut. The gentleman he'd been raised to be bellowed from deep inside.

"She gives all the airs of a lady, Mr. Fitzgibbons, not a tavern wench to be thrown over my shoulder and ravished."

"Na tha' you were the type for that, sir," the first mate agreed. "But now might be the time ta be considerin' it."

Trent stared at the maps, done with the conversation. He waved the man away and tried to plot his course and prayed that didn't include the beautiful lady below.

Chapter Eleven

THE ROOM WAS DARK, LIT only by the fireplace. The bustle of patrons and ladies of questionable repute fluttered around him but James didn't notice them. The chatter and the clinking of glasses were barely audible as he clutched the brandy glass and stared into the flames, his mind numb, his heart aching beyond any injury he had ever had. Where was she?

Today marked six weeks since she disappeared. Six. His mind was worn out from the search, his nerves wracked, his body exhausted. Sleep was a distant memory, dreams long gone. But the drive moved him forward—find her and bring justice wrecking from the heavens to those who had taken her from him.

"There you are, ole chap."

James blinked, breaking his stare at the fire. He glanced up to Clearwater standing next to him, a grin spread across his face.

"Yes, I'm here. Where else would I be at this time of the day?" he grumbled. Being at the club was his refuge from the house that was way too large and too vacant for him to stand.

James sat back in his chair, balancing his glass of the amber liquor between both hands, and studied his friend. "May I ask why you are here, with me, in a club with all the other married men, counting the soiled doves, instead of pursuing a lady to court?"

"Posh!" Clearwater downed a gulp from his glass. "I have found my lady."

"Truly? Congratulations are in order." He tipped his glass. "So where is our future Lady Clearwater?"

His friend's eyes darted toward the flames, away from James. "She is pre-occupied this evening. A trip out of the city. Family, I believe. I will join her shortly." He smiled.

"Very good." James decided Clearwater's distant look was one of missing the girl, whoever she was. But now was not the time to worry for his friend. He had Eleanor. He finished his drink and set the glass down. "I think I shall go visit our friends in the gaol, see if they have any more knowledge to spill." He clenched his fists, expecting it might take persuasion, or more of a way to vent steam because he doubted any more could be learned.

Clearwater followed suit. "Good. I believe it would be a much more enjoyable pastime verses flat champagne and giggling damsels." He set his glass down. "Shall we?"

∞

THE SEA WAS BEAUTIFUL. ELLE simply could not believe she had missed it all her life. Well, she could only imagined she missed it as her faulty memory didn't seem to recall any occurrence with it. She sighed. Lacking a past was annoying but there was something about the lull of the waves, the bright sun, and air that seemed so clean and invigorating. It soothed her soul. Almost like this was a new beginning in her life. She began to relax.

Perhaps this was God's way for her, to belong on the seas. She breathed deep, taking in the salty freshness of the air and gaze out over the ocean.

Behind her, the bustle of the ship as the men completed about their chores. She knew without looking that Cavendish was on the upper deck. That was where she always found him. He left her alone and the few run-ins they had, he'd been coarse or rude with her. He acted mad at her. She didn't understand why. She tried to stay out of his and everyone else's way. Even now, she stood near the back of the ship, in an alcove that wasn't out in the open for all to gawk at her, for the men still did, regardless how many days she had been there. And at night, she ate alone in the cabin, slept alone there, too. In many ways, that should relieve her, to be alone, but it also made her feel like she had the plague or something worse. And that thought disturbed her more.

One thing had changed last night. Cavendish had come to the cabin. She had been asleep. But when he tried to enter quietly, he banged the door on the chair she'd placed nearby to warn her of an intruder. She didn't move on the cot but clutched the knife Fitzgibbons had handed to her days ago. "To keep as a warning to other varmints," he'd advised her. But the captain didn't come near her. He'd rearranged the chair closer to the desk, plopped himself into it, his feet resting on the desktop. Out of the corner of her eye, she saw him prop his hat over his eyes and try to sleep.

His presence didn't allow her to return to slumber. Instead, her heart started an erratic thumping and the heat rose inside her. She wanted to throw off the bed sheet but at the same time, didn't want to draw attention. With her mouth turning dry, she watched him through slitted gaze that roved over his whole body. Even in a supposedly relaxed state, he gave an essence of power and strength. And something else. Something that made a shimmer course through her, sending off sparks deep inside her. Her breasts tingled, and the core of her being turned to liquid that pulled with desire. It wasn't right nor normal, she berated herself. He mourned for his wife and perhaps she was spoken for, as well. But the truth eluded her. She bit her bottom lip, holding her breath. Why on earth had he returned to the cabin, when every other night he left her alone? And during the day, he avoided her except when he had no choice. It was very frustrating.

Staring out at the sea, she realized she was no longer angry at him. She was angry at herself. Her attraction to him was growing. If she could just quiet the warning tone, no matter how faint it was, she might enjoy it, for she was almost certain he was attracted to her, too. Or he hated her.

It was this musing that kept her thoughts occupied and it took the bristling of the hair on the back of her neck to bring her back to now. She didn't move but warily glanced about. At her location, no one should be able to surprise her. She was closer to the back of the decking, to where the ship's captain's cabin sat. More or less, nestled into a corner, she felt safe until now.

"Aye thar, lassie."

The voice behind her shot an icy shiver down her spine. She stiffened but didn't turn, instead she let her hand that casually crossed her waist find the hilt to the knife that rested inside her waistband.

A hand snaked around her. His fingers caressed her cheek and down her neckline.

"Wha' a beauty ta be lef alone," he whispered.

Fear fought to control her but something deep inside her screamed she would not be taken again. Without a

basis to why she thought this had happened before, she
sprung into action, gripping the knife firmly, withdrawing it and spinning toward her attacker in one swift move.
Her swipe found a mark, slicing through his forearm. He
yelped, whipping his injured arm back but grabbing a fist-
ful of hair.

"Ain't she cooperatin', Gene?" another man whose
voice she didn't recognize asked.

Gene yanked her head back and brought his own knife
to bear, the blade pressed against her throat. "Aye, she be
a fightin' type, which be one o' me fav'rites," he claimed,
his mouth close to her ear.

She couldn't see the varmint who held her but the
other one was right before her and she recognized him.
He grinned with his toothy smile, spittle glistening down
his greasy beard.

"Aye, Gene, fightin' wenches are th' best cunt." His
hand jetted out, fingers looped into the v-opening on
her blouse, ripping the material down and quickly snaked
inside to grab her breast, squeezing it tight.

Elle screamed as her knee jacked up, right into the man's
groin and her weapon hand whipped back, stabbing the
one who held her in him. Both men grunted, doubling
over, the one behind her releasing her. She spun and held
the knife out in front of her, her feet spread to steady herself for their attack.

"I'll not be manhandled," she snarled, "not by you or
any other!"

More pirates appeared at the commotion. None of them
moved to help their brethren but neither did they move
to take her. It was as if they all had never seen a woman
use a knife in defense before. But then again, neither had
she…when did she learn to defend herself? The mystery
of who she was continued to confound her.

Trent spat into the cuspidor again. The rum he tried to swallow was bitter-tasting, just like his mood. Of course, that woman was the cause.

"You be a mite foul, this bonny morn." Fitzgibbons stood to the side, taking a step back as the spit hit the side of the vessel.

"Lack of slumber does that," he grumbled. When the first mate's brow shot up in a questioning manner, he added, "I did as you suggested. I went to my cabin last night, to 'claim her', so to speak, but I could not sleep." He cursed again.

"Aye, but ya be feelin' a wee bit better for havin' done so, right?"

"Hardly. The men were fighting this morning because there are pieces missing from our last haul." He ran his fingers through his mussed hair before jamming the hat back on. "Many of the men believe she is bad luck, or worse, a witch, who stole it because they can't find the missing treasure."

Fitzgibbons frowned. "Just what of it is missin'?"

He shook his head. "According to the watch, the quartermaster's book reads there are ten more pieces of eight and a bag of rubies, emeralds, and diamonds worth two thousand pounds sterling. They think it's her because it is small and could be made into jewelry." He pinched the bridge of his nose. "Damn woman is wrecking havoc that I can't afford to have. So I've decided we are heading to London to deposit her arse and make the men not feel so cursed. As to the missing pieces, that is a mystery and one we will solve."

The first mate stared at him hard. "You donna truly

believe the lass capable of stealing? We've had watch on it since that raid."

That comment grated his nerves, simply because he knew the man was right. "What would you have me do? In the name of the saints—"

A scream rang across the deck, stopping everyone in their tracks. Trent tensed. It was her. Trent scanned the deck, looking for her. Where the hell was she?

He found the crowd forming toward the back of the ship and he growled. Fitzgibbons said something but Trent never heard him, leaping over the railing and landing on the deck below. In a few long strides, he got to the mess of men and wheedled his way through. What he found brought him to a dead stop. Elle stood, her shirt ripped, the gaping hole hinting at the ample breasts that were beneath it. Her hat was on the ground, her bundled hair askew, as if someone had grabbed it. The mere thought of that goaded the animal inside him into a roar, demanding those who'd attempted to ruin his mate die for their offense. He pushed closer and was shocked.

Two pirates were before her. One curled on the deck, whimpering in pain as he rocked, his hands covering his crotch. The other gripped his arm tight against his waist, the other hand grasped over his upper arm. A smattering of blood was on the deck. The knife in her hand still pointed toward them. He busted through to her side.

"Show is over! Back to work!" The pirates mumbled but turned to go back to their jobs. Trent glared at her. "Where the hell did you get that?"

Her eyes widened. "How dare you! Your men attacked me!"

He slid his gaze from her to Fitzgibbons, who wore a half grin upon his mouth. His gaze darted back to her. She was trouble. He swore under his breath.

He snarled at Gene and his anguishing cohort. "What were you two up to?"

"Nothin', sir," Gene snapped back. His companion nodded, mumbling the same.

Trent rolled his eyes. The tension in the air was thick enough for a knife to cut through it and with that analogy in his head, he snagged the weapon from the girl's hand. She gasped, her surprise mixed with anger and pain while she rubbed her palm. Perhaps he had been too forceful but... In an instant he turned to the two sailors with the blade pointed at them.

"Just what caused this incident? Or shall I pry the blade into you to find the truth?"

Instantly, both men turned peaked, Gene more so than the other pirate. "She was just standin' here, all lone like," Gene argued. "Pretty as a new shillin' and got no ben'factor, sir. Just thought maybe she'd take a likin' to us..."

"Not bloody likely!" the girl snapped back.

Trent was on the verge of laughing at her reaction, though he oscillated from wanting to agree she was evil to wanting to cut the heart of both Gene and the other, who's name escaped him. Where the hell did this pirate sign up for his ship? He pinched the bridge of his nose again, squeezing his eyes shut. This must be hell.

"You do realize most of the men think you are also a thief or witch, depending." He wanted to gauge her reaction to that accusation, believing he knew the answer but had a flicker of doubt.

A look of shock stole her words away. She gulped. He watched her throat bob as she swallowed. Her slender neck looked exquisite as the apple slowly lowered. His cock twitched. It irritated him and amused him that she could do this to him. But his rational thinking won. She had to go.

"A witch? Ha! If that stood the case, do you not think I would've found my way home?" Her face was flush with anger, her blue sapphire eyes ablaze. "And thief? Look at me! Do I sport anything of value? You gave me the clothes, for all that stands holy! What did I steal? You accuse me? You are all pirates, for pity's sake!"

She was alive and so vibrant. It made her more beautiful and was in awe, for a moment. But as the silence thickened, his own fear of her grew. He realized he was growing too fond of her and that could not be allowed. He was in mourning and seeking vengeance, how dare he be attracted to another. It was the devil's work!

"You took from our last haul," he countered. His voice was steady and sure. He was now in agreement with his men that somehow she had cast a spell on them. "Treasured pieces small enough not to be noticed at first, but worth more than the bulk of the take."

Her lips thinned as she obviously fought to retain more foul language. Pity, he thought. She gave an harrumph to curses like no one else.

"And where would I keep such pieces?" she challenged.

A shiver raced down his spine at the very thought that she invited him to search her. But before he could say a word, she spied the crew that had now drifted back to the perimeter to watch the show. Knowing that as they sailed on the sea, she could not escape. He didn't move but watched as she scanned the pirates. He hoped the humiliation might make her tell him where the items where but as the seconds mounted, he decided to give his men the peace they wanted.

"It does not matter." He cleared his throat. "The ship will return to London, where we will release you."

She spun to face him. "Before you decide to do so, perhaps you'd like to know who your real culprits are, for I know they took your treasure." A tight but smug smile came to her now controlled face. The type only ladies of the ton could master, he recalled.

"No, we leave for England." He'd had enough. She was bad luck. He had a mission. His men wanted treasures. She stood in the way. It was time to take the thief/witch/seductive siren and leave her to where she could not distract him. He strode away, pleased with his decision.

"No! Wait! You do have thieves here! Ones who look to take and have you overthrown as captain!"

He stopped. Her voice was frantic, pleading and sincere. Pirates were a difficult lot. That he knew. He was captain because of what he could offer them in hauls, and the bigger the better. Any leader could be voted out. Pirates were more democratic and liberal than the colonies. He shook his head. It was possible, in his hunt for Rachel's killer, he might have missed discontentment.

"What are you talking about?"

"There are men who decided they deserve more than you allot out." She squared her shoulders, but there was a haunted look in her pleading eyes. He came to her and took her arm and steered her toward his cabin.

"How do you know? When?" His voice lowered, to try to keep the conversation between them. She walked slowly, aware the rest of the crew paused, hoping to hear.

"See the two standing up there? The one who wears the red bandana and the man next to him?"

Trent straightened and took a glance on the railing surrounding the lower deck. He found the two. "Yes. Carlos and Pedro. Joined the crew last season. Decent pirates, take ball and chain with the rest of us if captured, they have fared equally in our hauls."

"They believe they deserve more," she stated. "In fact, they complained they have lacked a proper portion and decided they'd amend that discrepancy with the last."

They rounded the corner to his cabin, Fitzgibbons in tow. Once inside the room, he frowned. "And they said all of this, with you present? If this is true, why didn't they take you as prize?"

She gasped at his accusation. If it had been him unhappy with the arrangement, he would have swooped her up in a heartbeat, her beauty making her a priceless item to men who haven't seen even a lowly woman in weeks. Even in his assessment of her as a treasure made his body tense, a shiver washing through him. Fitzgibbons's harrumph returned him to now. He coughed, but reality struck him hard. The woman was getting under his skin. That he could not afford!

With a small but audible gulp, her tongue licked her bottom lip before she could speak. "They didn't see me." She stood silent, shifting on her feet. "They spoke a language that wasn't English but, apparently, I understood it." She shrugged, confusion in her eyes.

"It wasn't French, by chance?"

She shook her head. "No, I'd recognize French, I believe. This, at first, I didn't understand, but it wasn't Français."

He turned to his first mate. "What do you say? Do they speak the tongue of the West Indies? And where did we pick them up?"

The Irishman chuckled. "I believe in one of the Spanish isles, likely Hispaniola."

"Yes!" She jumped. "It was Spanish."

He blinked. "That language isn't usually taught to the English lords or ladies. Or in London. So where did you learn that?"

∞

ELLE STRAINED HER MIND TO dig through the vines that barred her memory. Glimpses of a woman, dressed in stern clothes, came to her thoughts. She triggered a faint memory of direction and guidance, like a governess. The woman was strict yet loving.

"Someone from your past?"

She still gazed at the distant past, not yet focusing back in the present. "Yes. From my childhood. She watched over me. Isabella, I believe was her name. She was Spanish." She smiled larger as that memory fought to be heard.

Trent snorted. "Glad a part of your past is dawning." He turned toward Fitzgibbons. "Bring Carlos and Pedro here and let us see what they have to say."

As the first mate left, Trent motioned for her to follow him outside the cabin. Gladly, she did, pleased to be out in the cooler temperature the open decking had, even doused in sun, over the enclosed cabin. Taking a breath of the fresh air, she closed her eyes, hoping the one thread of memory that came to of her governess would set other strands to show themselves. But as the seconds past and nothing more came. She bit her lower lip in frustration.

Within minutes, the first mate shoved the two pirates across the deck, both grumbling and dragging their feet. Trent waited a moment for them to quiet before he began.

"I have heard through the crew that certain items off the last bounty have gone missing. Small but highly valuable pieces."

At first, neither moved but then Carlos spat, "Yes, and the lady there is a witch, damning all of us on this ship. Word goes she paid the devil with those jewels to aid in our destruction."

Trent's eyes widened the same moment Elle's jaw dropped open. She was now a witch?

"I am not a witch!"

"Shush." The captain clutched his hands behind his back and paced before them. "Interesting point, sirs, is the fact that you two only recently joined us here on the *Equuleus*, am I not correct?"

Neither answered but Pedro shuffled, his head low.

"What has tha' ta do with this?" Carlos threw back, his jaw tense.

Trent stared at Pedro. About his waist was a sash, tightly wrapped around his middle and tucked in at the side. It also bulged there, more so than the fabric required. Elle bet he was hiding something and hoped the captain pushed.

Instead, he continued his pacing. "Did you not come from Hispaniola?"

Carlos frowned. "Yes."

"Under the Spanish crown?"

Juan finally spoke. "Many places in the West Indies are ruled by the Spanish."

"Yes, and do you not speak that tongue more fluently than English?" He stopped right before Pedro.

"Yes."

Trent pointed to the sash. "Hand that over to me."

Both men took a step back. "That is me personable stuff, sir." Pedro's hand instantly covered the bulge.

Trent nodded and Fitzgibbons snatched out to retrieve the pouch from where he stood, behind the two. Pedro turned, his face beet red.

"That ain't yours ta be takin'!"

But the bag was in Trent's hands and he promptly opened it to find gold coins and a few gems. "I somehow doubt you owned this prior to the last raid."

"Ya donna know what we possess!" Carlos pressed.

"The lady heard you speak, claiming you decided you two were more qualified to have more than the rest of the crew, including me."

At that statement, both men tensed and lunged forward for a fight. Elle sidestepped and leaned back as Pedro aimed for her. Fitzgibbons's first hit his jaw, swinging the pirate's head to the side and he fell hard on the deck. Trent ducked Carlos's swing and came up at him, a knife in his hand. He pressed the pirate against the cabin's outer bulwark, blade against his throat. Carlos's color drained as the knife lodged into the fold of his neck without slicing.

"Mr. Fitzgibbons, have these two thrown into the lower cell. We will rid ourselves of them shortly."

"Aye, aye, Capt'n."

As the two were hauled off by two pirates the first officer hailed over, Trent pulled one of the gold coins from the pouch and handed it to Elle.

"I believe you have earned a share of the treasure."

She took the Spanish coin and twirled it with her finger, a thrill racing through her as she played with the gift from him. Perhaps she meant more to him than she thought and that pleased her. The piece sparkled in the sunlight. The entire spectacle had her thoughts jumbled with joy and frustration. A piece of her past had come to light but nothing more than a hint of what and who she was. A low hiss escaped her lips at how the door to the past opened but closed just as rapidly.

As to the pretty coin in her hand, another thought crossed her mind—was she now a pirate, having stolen goods?

∞

FITZGIBBONS WATCHED HER STARE AT the gold piece, the look of amazement on her face. As her hand fisted around it and she shoved it into the pocket of her pants, he smiled. That one item was worth thousands in pound sterling, he'd wager, but her aid and her beauty paled the item.

"What is that look for?"

He turned to find the captain glaring at him and he couldn't help but snort because he knew the response before he asked it.

"So, you still be thinkin' the girl is bad luck? Enough so to take the risks, considerin' the latest catch here, to sail back the Thames and leave her?"

Trent's jaw twitched and it made him smile bigger.

"Of course not," Trent replied with a sigh. "She was admirable on this, despite the fear others have about her. Look about the ship now," he motioned. "Those men have grins and nods directed toward her for disposing these thieves and miscreants. They will be easy to unload on one of those nameless outcroppings just north of France. Let them find their own way to hell. But her?" He shook his head as if in disbelief. "I fear not only the risk is too great to return her, but worse, as the men would pin me down for getting rid of the bad charm that is good."

Fitzgibbons smiled. The girl needed to stay, if only to grant Trent peace, despite his claim he didn't desire her. Only a fool would believe that.

As if reading his mind, Cavendish gave him a hard glare and muttered, "Get that grin off your face. She's still bad luck, in more ways than not. But she has earned a right to sail with us for now. And once her memory returns in full, we may all regret this decision, for I'll swear by God Almighty, she is a lady of the realm and not a pirate's wench. We'll all pay for keeping her here, despite whatever fear she has of returning home." He spat and walked away.

The first mate wanted to laugh. The only one who'd pay was Cavendish and that would be he lost his heart to the beauty.

Chapter Twelve

BUZZZZZZ

James swatted another fly away as if it was nothing and took sip from the cheap gin. He watched with minor amusement as Clearwater beat at one near him, only managing to slap his cheek instead, quickly followed by a somewhat muted curse.

"Was it truly a wise decision to frequent such a..." Clearwater's gaze darted as his lips curled in a grimace. "Filthy place?"

James sat back in the creaky wooden straight chair and snorted. He had to admit wondering the same thing. Even as they sat there today, he halfway expected the chair, one of the only chairs as most of the tables had benches, to collapse underneath him.

"You recall what those creatures said," referring to the two sailors questioned in regards to Eleanor's disappearance.

"You mean, that dribble they confessed? Yes, I do and remember quite clearly their blood spitting on the floor after you pounded them to get more information. Truly, understandable. I, too, would seek blood for stealing Eleanor, but what a ghastly appearance they made!" He shivered.

James couldn't help but grin at the comment. He had spirited to the docks and found the two men scared half-witless when he stormed them into gaol, his sword lashed to his side. One way or another, he was going to get them to spill more information and figured if fear of a nobleman, especially one armed with a blade, didn't do it, he'd resort to cutting off their fingers, or worse. The two understood him plainly enough and words flowed from their mouths like a river over a rocky bed, halfway confusing and contorted. But the basis was, she had somehow escaped and the last they saw, she ran from them at breakneck speed and to not be caught, jumped aboard a ship. After more cajoling, they spit out a name that took the Runner a few minutes to find—the *Equuleus*. A ship for a privateer named Cavendish.

They ran a quick search and discovered the ship pulled from anchor immediately thereafter with no one appearing to know her course. James collapsed right there, every ounce of energy—and hope—dashed.

"James, ole man, I realize you are hurting and want vengeance but that ship left just over a month or so ago." Clearwater reached out and grasped James wrist, squeezing it. "I am sorry. You may never find her again."

James's vision blurred, as he too knew it was a lost cause in many respects but he loved her too much to give up hope.

"I do not believe that." He inhaled deep, straightening in his chair, ignoring the shifting it did under his seat. He grabbed his mug and downed the rest of his gin, or the concoction they claimed was gin. Clearwater would never understand, he knew it. His friend, though, still stayed at his side, to help him if she was found, or worse. He shuddered at that thought.

"This is the most vile stuff I've ever tasted." Clearwater put his mug down, his lips twisted in disgust.

Clearwater was right. "Granted, but it's the best of the house." James halfway shrugged. "But if I can pick up any news on the *Equuleus*, then all the swill in England is worth it."

Silence passed with Clearwater staring at him. James wasn't sure if the flash he saw in his friend's eyes registered too much other than thinking his friend was insane. At this point, he wondered that himself. She'd been gone too long, creating an emptiness in him that was unbearable. He'd rather die than give up on finding his love.

The half-rotten door to the pub creaked open and the sunlight poured in, lighting up the dirt and grime of the room. Most of the patrons looked away or shielded their eyes from the bright light. A shadow broke the glare as two more men stumbled into the dark room. James kept a watch on them without moving his seat. The two sailors were barefoot, their pants torn at the bottom of the leggings, and their billowy shirts gave the marks of being worn for days. Men from the sea and ones that were not happy. That intrigued James and he tilted his head to try to hear them as they slid into a table off to the side. What he heard was grumbles and curses laced with anger.

"...who tha hell does he think he be?" the taller one spat. "How dare he be leavin' us out in tha mid of nowhere!"

The other one nodded furiously as the pub wench sauntered up, toting two mugs of gin. The complainer gave her a toothy smile.

"Thanks." He took one of the mugs. His companion took the other one, nodding in agreement with him. As she left, their conversation dropped to barely audible. In fact, the only thing James could hear was their downing the liquor. He closed his eyes, counting slowly. This shack was the nearest to the docks, the one those two abductors ranted they had met the man "his lor'ship". The man who hired them to take Eleanor. He planted himself here every evening, downing this horrible gin, dressed in his worse clothes—ones that still looked vastly better than anyone else wore in the tavern—and waited for another clue to where Eleanor was.

"...as if Cavendish owned the damn seas!"

Clearwater shot a glance to him from across the table. "Did you hear?"

James bent his head slightly, to appear that there was something on the table he found more interesting, curtailing his inclination to jump up. But he couldn't stop the way his lips curled up.

"Finally."

"Thanks to the Lord!" Clearwater proclaimed. "An end to dreary hours with rancid swill." He raised his mug in toast and gagged as he swallowed the gin.

James smirked but kept his attention more on the two across the room, contemplating how to approach them.

"...that witch drove him, you know tha'," one complained.

The other nodded. "How're we ta know she got Spanish?"

James nearly jumped, his heart beating rapidly. Eleanor confided she had a governess who was from Spain and taught her the foreign tongue. Considering the war, and Spain under control of France, it wasn't a fact she wanted anyone to know. French, after all, remained the diplomatic language and many ladies learned it. But Spanish? No.

"Yeah, betcha he's got'er cunt, too, ta control her, too." He spat on the floor.

That statement zeroed in to James. Eleanor? Not only with a pirate ship but in bed with the captain? His blood roared, the pounding in his ears deafening, Clearwater comments drowned out by it. It couldn't be true! Not his wife, not his love! His free hand clenched, his other tightened around the pottery mug, the pain of it branching through his hand and up his wrist.

"Pretty tart." The other sailor chuckled before his face turned hard. "But we done lost what coin we had! Now we gotta find another ship. He dumped us to where that'd not be happenin' soon. Here ain't no better." He moaned.

"I says we find one that'll let us find tha bastard and take back what's ours!" the first pirate declared and promptly burped.

"And maybe be taken that wench, too. Thinkin' we teach 'er true Spanish ways." He winked at his friend and both gave a hideous, evil laugh.

It was that laugh that launched James upright.

"James!" Clearwater hissed.

James huffed but knew his friend was curtailing his desire to slug those two to the ground for their remarks. In reality, he knew Clearwater was right to stop him. It would do neither him nor Eleanor any good to pulverize these two without finding more information. He paused and redirected his thoughts. The saucy serving wench gave him a wayward smile. In return, he motioned for her to come over.

Bouncing across the dark and grimy room, she slid next to him, arriving after he settled back down to his chair. He gave her a smirking grin, trying to be nonchalant.

"What can I git you, gov'nor?" she asked, her own smile genuine.

"Petunia, do you see those two sailors across the way?"

She grunted. "Aye. Riff raffs of the *Equuleus*, Captain

Cavendish's ship. They were thieves aboard, so he dumped them at sea." She shrugged. "They managed to convince a sailor to pick them up to return 'em here, so they be claimin'."

A perfect set up for him to utilize, and James would exploit it to the hilt. He pulled Petunia closer. "Sweet Petunia, I want you to bring them a round of this place's best drink."

She stared at him, her eyes wide but he gave her his best smile as he slipped a coin into her hands. Her fingers grasped the piece and she bit on it to believe it was real silver, not wood and smiled as it passed the test. She tilted her pretty head and gave him a return grin. "Sure nuff, guv," she chirped and spun to get the order.

"So, what's your plan, ole man?" Clearwater muttered.

James watched the two out of the corner of his eye. Petunia delivered the mugs, giving a laugh to the two along with a few words. Whatever she said got them to glance over toward him. He raised his cup and gave them a nod. Their reaction, returning the gesture, was exactly what he'd hoped for but he schooled his thoughts and emotions to remain calm. He needed that so his next move would not set them off from his questions. As the bar wench wandered away, he gave Clearwater a nod and got up. His friend followed.

"Gents," James started, fighting hard not to laugh at the word. "Did I overhear you correctly about the *Equuleus*?"

The taller of the two wiped the back of his hand across his mouth. "Aye. What's it to ya?"

James hit pay dirt. "I'd like to ask you a few questions. It appears, it's captain stole an," he paused and gave Clearwater a quick glance, "item of great expense from me. A jewel."

"What's it worth ta ya?" the other stuttered but the

interest was in his eyes.

"Its worth more than you can make in a single haul."

They grumbled with disbelief so he ordered another round, utilizing every method to soften them up. He pulled up a rickety chair and plopped into his seat with a smile. Yes, all the days of waiting were about to be redeemed.

"A FTA YOU, MILADY." THE PIRATE stepped back and motioned her before him.

It was an odd set of circumstances. Elle's unlucky status miraculously turned to being treated like a queen since she exposed Juan and Roberto as the cutthroats and thieves they truly were. She wanted to laugh, since pirates were just that, but these two stealing from the crew and plotting to oust Trent placed them just a step beyond the rest. No one would ever trust them and in the world of pirates, that was a death sentence, or so Trent informed her.

But still being treated like a lady, out here in the middle of the ocean on a ship full of thieves just was unusual.

She scanned the horizon and found the outline of an island ahead. Trent informed her they would stop there and pick up supplies before crossing the sea to the Americas. The island lay off the coast of North Africa and reported to be lush and beautiful, something the crew needed before thrusting off to the West Indies. That long two month passage would prove difficult, Trent told her, if the men didn't have a place to relax. The land may be gorgeous but what the men wanted was the access to booze and whores that serviced sailors there.

"Looks strange, does it not? To see land again," Trent said softly, standing behind her.

"A touch," she answered, nodding. "Almost as if it's an

illusion." She turned to face him. "My world has been confined to this ship and the men who sail her."

He chuckled, his glaze boring into her. "Makes one feel safe, does it not? To be able to see everything that is in your grasp, know the space, and what is and isn't there. Land, though, means the same to a sailor—confining, almost like a prison. The open sea is freedom." He shrugged.

She smiled, trying to understand but with the bulk of her past still locked away from her, she had nothing to base anything on. The reflection on his face showed he understood her undecidedness and she blushed at being so telling.

He leaned back against the railing next to her. "Still nothing more?"

She shook her head. She hated to admit it. Even her dreams were void of anything other than being at sea. She was sure that being on the water wasn't normal for her but nothing else came to mind. The mere recognition of that tripped her heart into a fast pounding pace and she panted as a frantic frenzy washed through her.

He took her hand and squeezed it. "Breathe. All is well."

His voice was low and soft. She locked gazes with him. His brown eyes sparkled in warmth, yet teasing dance. Somehow, this pirate made her feel good. Comfortable. But still, she needed more.

"Since the..." she paused. "The men appear more... polite towards me. How is it I went from a bad omen to courtesy and manners?"

He chuckled again, and reaching out with his fingers, lightly brushed the line of her cheek, down to her jawline. His eyes were dark, almost black in color.

"You exposed the men who thought they could take more than they earned, and thwart the mission this ship has launched over. While they are not completely thrilled

with the idea of a woman aboard, they are also a super-
stitious lot, believing you are good over evil. And to get
rid of you would impair them from future prizes by bad
luck." His forefinger touched her lips. It was ever so light,
she almost didn't feel it. With a puzzled look, he turned
to walk away.

The loss of his touch was coldness. Somewhere deep
inside her, a longing for him had settled in, but to have his
touch only to leave left her feeling abandoned. Instantly,
she spoke, an attempt to return his attention back to her.

"And how do you feel, Captain?"

He stopped and slowly turned to face her. "I still believe
you are dangerous, in more ways than you could imagine,
and some of that is to yourself. Your real self could be bad
or good, but we've no clue at this point. While returning
you to England might have proved the better part of valor,
I believe the men would've refused to sail there, outside
the reason of them being hung as pirates. So I find myself
in a quandary of do I find a British ship or town in the
West Indies that'll take you or keep you at my side, for
more fortune."

A chill swept through her at the mere idea of returning
her to England. "But you wouldn't return me now, would
you? You dropped the Spanish at that island off the coast
of France. We've sailed for four days so to return there
would burn more fuel and deplete your supplies."

At her rational, yet quick, argument against reversing
back to England, Trent laughed loudly. "On that you are
correct, my lady. Pirates can be lazy, when allowed, and to
see England now, when more fortunes lay ahead, they no
doubt would refuse to do." He took her hand more fully
into his and pulled her closer. "Instead, I'd like to show
you how the sea can be beautiful." He raised her hand to
his mouth for a kiss.

Where his lips touched her skin, a fire burned, quickly spreading up her arm. Her body tightened and her core burned. He was so handsome, this rugged daredevil man who posed as a pirate but held the manners of a gentleman. Often, she thought to ask him where he learned such courtesies but she didn't. She just couldn't decide why. Something hit a cord, a feeling mixed a memory she couldn't visualize. It scared her, but she concentrated on him and how he touched her. Whatever her past was, she had to let that frustration go and simply glow in his light. But what if it went further?

Chapter Thirteen

THE FEMININE LAUGHTER FLOATED UP the stairs. James forced himself to sit still in the armchair and wait. The room hadn't changed much since the last time he saw it. Still decorated in frills and lace, Lydia's bedchamber matched her—lovely, feminine, and excessive all at once. But his dalliance with her was years ago, brief, thankfully. A lady who wanted it all and could hide it behind a façade of innocence. It made his stomach twist.

Mounting anger drove him to her townhouse even though it was late. He shoved his way in, right past the butler who stood speechless, and right up the staircase to her room. The door swung wide open and he was greeted with—nothing. A garbled curse escaped his mouth as he kicked at the step stool before the fireplace chair. Running his hands through his hair, he concentrated on thinking. The discussion with those two vermin at the gin joint had revealed more than he hoped for…but with a price he didn't want to accept.

How the hell would he get her back from a man who controlled a pirate ship? That was, if he could find them.

And that was when Lydia came to his mind... So he found his way here, though he didn't remember the journey, his thoughts were wrapped in red fury at the complications.

The doorway cracked with a sound of her giggle accompanying it. Inside she stepped, still dressed in her ball gown of the evening, and at her side was a tall, blond-haired lord in tow.

The two of them didn't see him, nor did she care that her servants knew she was home alone with a man this late at night or that another sat in her bedroom alone waiting for her. Echoes of his past with her of a similar time, she lured him to her bed, played in his mind. There was an air around her that somehow, she was above the rules of society. It had attracted him at first, and now, made him want to shake his head. Even now, he saw she hadn't changed and that was precisely why he sat here, waiting for her. At her age, she should curb her tastes, he thought. But her infectious laughter only demonstrated how that'd never work.

She spun on her heel, removing her shawl when her gaze fell upon him, bringing all her laughter to a halt.

"Lord Windhaven, what an unexpected surprise." Her tone was a mixture of surprise, shock, weariness, and sat-isfaction. Satisfaction that he was here, in her bedroom. He almost rolled in the mere thought that his trip had nothing to do with her expectations.

He ignored her and glared at her companion. "Lord Hillwood, I expect you have other things to do right at this moment."

The young man's shoulders jerked back, his face paled a bit when he saw James.

"Lydia, I mean, my lady, I believe Lord Windhaven is right and I must bow out unexpectedly..."

She whipped her head around to see him.

"...I apologize." He nodded toward James and backed out of the room.

When the door shut, again she spun toward him and stormed across the room. "How dare you!"

"He's below you, my dear," he commented drily.

"And you've come to your senses, seeking my attentions now?"

He was always amazed how quickly she could switch from anger to smitten as he witnessed the smile spread across her face while she sauntered over to him. Yet no matter how hard she tried, he had one thought, one motive to be in her bedchamber and it had nothing to do with seducing her. If nothing else, that fanned his initial reason.

As she bent to hug him, tilting her head, aiming to kiss him, he leaned back.

"I did not come for you."

A flash of anger passed over her face before she re-schooled her expression to an amiable smile. "Then what do I owe this invasion? One that pushes my beau out the door."

Her beau. That he knew was a lie. "Lydia, tell me about your father's business."

Her shoulders slumped as did her lower jaw. "My father's ownings? Why?"

The look in her eye told him everything. The only way he'd get anything out of her being a gentleman would never work. Her stance, the slant in her eye laid the rules—she'd tell him anything after he seduced her. His blood boiled. Eleanor's life depended on him to find her. As Lydia stood, her tongue licked her upper lip, trying to look alluring, the opposite happened and he exploded. He growled and rushed at her, pushing her up against the bedroom wall, his hand on her neck.

"This should be easy for you, since you're well acquainted with how to get men."

She gasped a strangled noise with his hand pressed against her windpipe.

"I can not fathom what you mean." Panic spreading across her face.

"You will tell me what you know of my wife's disappearance, Lydia." Anger twisted his gut. Eleanor's life hung in the balance. "Now!"

∞

ELLE STRETCHED. THERE WAS SOMETHING entirely decadent about sitting on the beach, her toes wiggling in the sand, her hair falling loosely about her shoulders and wearing no hat. The sunrays bathed her in pure light, the salt air filled her nostrils and the utter abandonment of sitting with nothing demanding her time—or her appearance—filled her with joy. This was what it was like to relax and she loved it.

"Is that a smile I see?"

Slowly she opened her eyes to Trent walking toward her from the palm trees that lined the beach.

"Perhaps," she replied, waiting for him to reach her. He was a handsome man, though not the type she believed she was used to being around. He wasn't pale like the veiled noblemen of London. In fact, he glowed as his face and hands were bronzed from hours in the sunlight aboard the ship. His walk was more like a saunter as he neared her, like a man looking for his next bedmate, his tight thighs visible in the leggings, his pull-over blouse loose and billowy in the sea breeze, giving her a hint of a muscular body that was hidden in clothes. She licked her lips and bit her lower one to bite back a moan. The man was trouble, sin in flesh. He was a pirate, a man driven by condemnation of whoever took his wife, so Fitzgibbons claimed, but he had the manners of a man of worth and a body of one who knew how to seduce. Elle's toes curled in the sand as he set her body to liquid again.

It just wasn't right, she knew that, but the reason never cleared other than he was married. A married man whose widowhood drove him to reckless abandon. That should stop her wanting him yet she knew, deep down, there was more. A voice of her inner core struggled to be heard, making her wonder if she, too, had a husband somewhere. And if so, where was he? It was a question and silence that ate at her, enough so to keep her distance from the Cavendish.

The longer the time went, the more tired she became of fighting to find out who she was.

With all the musing in her head, she didn't realize he had reached her until he plopped himself down on the sand next to her.

"For a lady who has been so demanding, the silence is deafening." He gave her another infectious grin and handed her a tin cup.

She laughed. "Can one not simply enjoy the view without conversing about it?"

He raised his eyebrows as he uncorked the dark brown bottle that had been in the crux of his arm a moment before. "Certainly. But I have yet to meet a member of the fairer sex who would remain quiet on purpose of her own choosing."

The smell of the rum as it poured into her cup tempted her to take a sip. Something told her this wasn't a liquor she'd tasted before.

"Perhaps you should be worried, then, for my silence. Who knows what I may be plotting."

"I would enjoy that worry, my sweet." He filled his cup

and shoved the bottle into the sand. Tipping his drink in the air, he said, "To your continued good health."

She nodded, lifting her cup in agreement then took a sip. She rather liked his use of the endearment of "my sweet". It unnerved her, making her stomach flutter. He hadn't done that before. But all thoughts came to a screeching halt as the rum burned its way down her throat. She wanted to gag at the first impact.

He gave her a knowing look over the rim of his cup. "I was about to tell you to sip it slowly."

When he reached for her cup, she snagged it back in her grasp, holding it against her chest. "No, its fine. I believe this is the first I've had of this liquor. It has a bite." And a warmth in her stomach that relaxed her more.

"I apologize. Rum is the local drink." He laughed. "I can find some wine—"

"No, truly. It tastes…" Her thoughts escaped her and her cheeks burned at the embarrassment of being lost in a sentence. "Exquisite. I'm sure I can adapt."

The pirate nodded and took another gulp of his drink.

She needed to stop staring at him so she downed another sip and dug her toes into the sand. "I think you have ruined me."

A chuckle was his answer but after a minute, he softly added, "And how would that be? A kiss does not make you wanton."

"But doesn't it, in a manner speaking?" She squirmed a little under his gaze but couldn't stop the rest of the words from falling out. "A lady, one with an injury, mind you, falls into your hands for protection yet you are hardly the type to do so, being a privateer who jumps into piracy. Meaning your loyalty and honor are questionable, considering the Crown gave you a letter of marque?" She gave him a slanted questioning look. He didn't answer. Didn't have to. "As I was saying, then you find yourself with a bad 'charm' aboard—a burden you stated no pirate would want. But you keep me when I exposed your men who were dishonorable to you. And me, with no memory I can recall correctly, I do not wear pants, walk barefoot, play in the sand with my toes and drink hard liquor."

"The fact that at this moment you do, does that make you unhappy?"

"No," she whispered. Her stomach flipped. This man made her crave for more, but what exactly that was, she feared to find out. The pull to him had grown and she hadn't decided if that was good or bad.

The silence threatened to overwhelm her. He had downed his cup and proceeded to refill it. She gulped the rest of hers and shuddered as the liquor burned a trail down to her stomach.

He raised his eyebrow. "More? I doubt you'll find that at any etiquette school, guzzling rum."

Her thoughts circled. Perhaps he was right but... "Yet, until I recall such an upbringing, I will indulge in one more." Retrieving her filled mug, she paused to look at him. "What of you? Are you not happy? And why would you turn on the English boats when the French are our enemy?"

⚬⚬

HER QUESTION HE SHOULD HAVE expected but he wasn't ready for it now.

The island sat just off the Mediterranean Sea, near North Africa. Its beauty had always captured his heart, after a grueling drive by his commander years ago when he was an officer in the HMS Navy. It was a time he had little fond memories of and one he abandoned as soon as his commission could be expired. Then, Rachel had changed his life and once more, he thought of this place. Even now, her ghost nudged him gently. He ignored it and refocused.

"I have my reasons." There, that was a simple enough answer. But the quizzical look on her face indicated otherwise. He couldn't help but drink in her beauty. Her hair glowed in the sunlight, her skin had a lovely sun-kissed hue from the voyage. Those stunning sapphire blue eyes danced, no doubt heated by the rum. Elle was like the treasure he always wanted but held just out of reach... That thought hit his gut and he wondered what had happened to him, to fall so easily for another when Rachel's death still needed to be atoned.

Yet, Elle was here and alive, beauty and attraction wrapped tightly in that perfect, petite form. His cock stirred and he shifted, uncomfortable for once with the lost lady who had no memory and had done nothing to lure him into her arms, but that was what he wanted. Mentally, he cussed.

"Mr. Fitzgibbons told me you lost your wife." She played with her bottom lip. He was furious at his first mate for speaking a word about Rachel and yet had an irresistible urge to kiss that beleaguered lip.

His member throbbed. He downed the rest of the rum in an attempt to drown the desire.

"Yes, I am a widower, thanks to pirates driven by higher stakes." There, he said it out loud.

Handing her cup to him to refill as he poured another for himself, she asked softly, "What happened, may I ask?"

He took another shot of the liquor, enjoying the spice and the burn. That heat spread throughout his body, unfortunately also accenting his hardened cock further. But he enjoyed the moment of relaxation without a care, when he knew better. Sitting on the beach, in the sunlight, the echo of the waves and seagulls filling the air and her beauty made him complete.

He blinked hard at the thought. There was still the vengeance that needed to be delivered. Staring out to the sea, he allowed the visions of Rachel, the ones he worked furiously to hide, filter back into his head. Her laughter reached out to him from the grave and that mere sound brought him back to the present.

"She was traveling to Rome, to where her parents resided. It was a trip she was familiar with, having made it other times, even during this conflict. The French have retained some of the courtesies of war, allowing passenger and merchant ships to pass unscathed." He forced his taut muscles to relax as he settled into the sand better. "But the one who lacked such manners flew the black and attacked, taking nothing more than live cargo of Rachel, my wife. Truly, it was odd. The luggage was left alone, the stores on the ship barely touched. All left as is. Except for her. They took her."

Elle's mouth dropped open but she remained silent, her attention on him alone.

With a deep breath, he continued. "There was no ransom, no demand for her return, just a jest of a note claiming she was with her rightful mate. Of course, I searched high and low. No word. So I found a ship, and since no one would let me commandeer their vessel for such, what they considered, 'outlandish ventures', I bought my own and scurried a crew out of docks. Not the type one would look for, but I didn't care. I needed to find her." He choked on the memory of the search, unable to talk. Memories of Rachel flooded his thoughts and the pit in his stomach grew, erasing his erection.

He made the mistake of looking into her eyes and found them awash in unshed tears. Her sympathy took his breath away.

With a deep breath, he continued. "It didn't take long for the news to find me." He paused, his heart squeezed at the memory. "She was found dead." His own eyes blurred when Elle's hand gripped his forearm.

"Oh, no," she whispered. "How awful. Why?"

He looked at her. The connection with her steadied him. With his free hand, he downed the rest of his drink.

"I do not know." He was still trying to understand what made no sense.

A tear fell down her cheek. "I'm so sorry."

It hit him, hard, in his gut. The pain. The anguish. Rachel. The loss of his love ripped at his gut, wanting to make him yell at the skies and to a God he doubted existed any more.

A cold, sobering cloak fell over him. "So now you know. That is what I've set out to find. Not gold, not riches, but the culprit for this crime. And I will make him pay!"

Chapter Fourteen

ELLE'S HEART BLED FOR HIM. What he told her was heartbreaking, to the point far beyond what the first mate hinted at. The need to comfort him pushed her forward to feel him, even if it was only her hand on his arm. Under her palm, his arm tensed and shuddered. His anger, frustration and despair reflected in his veiled eyes. But there was something about him, something that drew her closer, something she couldn't name and avoiding it was impossible.

So she tried the best she could to reach the man inside him, the one that, despite all the "misfortune" a lady brought to a ship and the threats the crew mumbled, protected her and kept her safe. She squeezed his arm, offering her sympathy and support.

He glanced at her.

"Did you bring her to this place?" It was a tentative question, a chance to find a tunnel out of his darkness. A darkness she'd witnessed on the last ship they violently attacked.

He gave her a half smile with a snort, as if grasping at

her offer. "No."

It turned quiet between them, as if they were under the cloud of doom. He'd not make her grieve for a woman she didn't know. Suddenly, he sat straighter and poured another round. She couldn't help but giggle, the warmth of the rum uncurling the tension inside her. Whatever produced it had the effect she'd hoped to get by any means—he chuckled, the dark cloud disappearing as he handed her cup back with a lopsided grin.

"I'd suggest you watch yourself," he warned. "'tis poison to those unaware."

"Poison? Rum?"

"Yes ma'am. Wait until morning to see."

She tilted her head at him. "How long are we here? To what purpose? What lays next?"

He leaned back in the sand, propped on his elbows. "My, are we not full of questions. I'm not sure I feel like discussing them."

Digging her toes into the sand, she wiggled them. This simple act opened a new sensation to her, the feel of the damp sand combined with the dry coat of the service. It drifted through the digits, gritted but silky. She kicked a small lump up, her lips curved in a halfway smile despite his lower mood.

"So for now, it is just us?" She shot him a sly glance. "You will be a gentleman."

He gave her a shake of his head but his look was roguish. "I'm a pirate." He winked. "A gentleman I am not." The rakish grin caused her to want his kiss. He was way too attractive, every move he made was like a god of the Ancient World, all muscles and fluid motion. Sitting within arm's reach of her made her nervous and excited. A bolt of energy rushed through her and she jumped upright, taking off in a run to the beach, laughter pouring from her. He made her feel alive and she loved it!

When she reached the water's edge, her toes dug into the wet sandy ocean bottom, the waves rolling in, the tiny shells and debris in the water abrading her feet and ankles. It was a sensation that invaded her, letting an inner self rejoice at the freedom she felt. The sunlight bathed her face, the sea breeze hugged her, and an inner liberty erupted, laughter announcing its arrival. She knew the pirate captain chased her and the glimpse she caught of him doing so, a smile on his face, made her soul soar.

She loped through the low water, her toes and heels hitting bumps on the sandy floor, small enough she ignored them as she plowed on, giggling. Then she hit a hard object, making her lose her balance but before she fell into the water, his strong, muscular arms wrapped around her middle, pulling her up. When her backside hit his rock hard chest, she gasped, the air escaping her lungs.

"Wait, my lady, let me," he whispered in her ear. His lips kissed the nape of her neck, just below that ear, sending shivers sparkling down her spine.

She could barely breathe, trembling in his arms. As he traced down her neckline then back up, her toes curled in the sand. Every part of her came alive, her nerves ricocheted down her limbs and reaching out to her nipples, which hardened to pebbles instantly. The linen blouse scratched her delicate hot spots. When he pulled her earlobe into his mouth, scraping it lightly with his teeth, a mewl escaped her lips.

It was like he could read her mind, her body's call for more was loud to her own ears. He turned her in his arms and locked his lips to hers, coaxing her mouth to part and letting his tongue invade. In response, she wrapped her arms around his neck and with her pelvis flush against his, the cradle of her groin wrapped around his hardened cock. Her lower lips were swollen and parted, as if knowing this was next. She had no recall of that but her body did, slowly rocking against him.

He moaned in her mouth as his tongue teased hers. She reveled in that when he suddenly pulled away and untucked her shirt, raised it to expose one of her breasts. The breeze of the ocean kissed her skin, making the already sensitive area go one step further and she wanted to scream for more. But she didn't have to ask before he answered her, taking her swollen nub into his mouth, his teeth grazing against her delicate skin. The feeling of it was a new height of ecstasy for her. She threw her head back and moaned loudly.

He chuckled against her nipple, the response sent a rippling sensation against her. He would undo her here, in the ocean front, at an island full of sailors. It was that notion that brought her back to her senses, and she struggled to find a way to stop him, a success done only after curbing her appetite, something she wasn't sure she had the strength to do.

"Stop! Please," she moaned. Or was it a groan? She didn't want him to stop but propriety told her this wanton behavior was not acceptable in public places—not that she thought this was inhabited or that the crew was close. It wasn't right. A small voice deep inside her screamed for her to stop, the sound drowned by the pounding of her heart.

Slowly, he gently pulled back, his breathing harsh and heavy. He looked into her eyes and she saw the darkness of hunger there, a type she bet matched her own.

"Apologies." His voice was rough. He tried to fix her shirt but his fingers fumbled with the material.

Still heated from inside, blood raced through her veins, she gave him a half smile and put her hands over his.

"Apologies are not needed. I am as guilty as you, throwing our selves over to passion." She cupped his face in her hands. The stubble of a distant shave scraped her palms. "You have yet to mourn properly. And me…" What of her? She searched again for a spark, a hint of her life prior to now but, again, her mind had a wall she couldn't climb. "I doubt I'm a soiled dove, given to desires. It's simply not done, not in the ton, nor here, the public display of intimate touch. Please forgive my wanton behavior."

He took her hands, gloved them with his own. "All is as it should be. You are a beautiful woman, Elle, the type that will turn a man's head, desires not long behind. Do not blame yourself. We shall continue, as if this never happened." He kissed the knuckles of one of her hands as he peeled it off his jawline.

She wasn't sure how happy she was with that statement yet when she gave him another glance, she was greeted with a warm smile and a twinkle in his eye. Oh, Cavendish was the type of man all women wanted but to give into him brought trouble indeed. Yet, the smile calmed her nerves and she returned it.

"Rum will take of the best of many a man," he continued, taking her by surprise and scooping her up in his arms as he walked back to the beach.

She didn't say a word but allowed herself the luxury of being in his arms, knowing that was as far as she could allow him to go. Deep down, a battle raged. She wanted him, her desires remained warm to her but that inner tongue struggled to be heard that she had no rights to this. If only she could figure out why…

JAMES STOOD, HIS FEET SLIGHTLY spread to keep him steady as the ship rode on the currents of the sea heading west, having left London five days ago. He was on the upper deck, not far from the captain of this ship called the *Olympus*, planted himself at a table, securing the maps with weights to prevent the wind whisking them away The captain plotted on the paper and yelled orders to his crew. James tuned the man out, no longer hearing his broken tongue as if the captain was going through puberty. Perhaps he was, James considered. When he hired this boy to captain this ship he'd 'borrowed' from Lydia for a trip, he didn't ask for age, but for experience. Whatever in blazes was his name? It'd come later, he mused. There was only one goal to be met and James would push them until they reached it—find Eleanor and find her fast. His hands fisted at his side, his gaze rarely leaving the skyline before them.

"I take it you think you can magically produce the West Indies on the horizon by staring hard enough at it, huh?"

James inhaled deeply, forcing his jaw to untighten. "No, just the waiting is slowly eating at me." He turned.

Clearwater had joined him for this journey, claiming he wanted to be there first hand when they seized the scoundrel who stole the lovely Eleanor. James appreciated his friend's companionship though he didn't understand why the man came. He needed to find a wife of his own and the Season was in full swing. Clearwater laughed it off, claiming he had a lady in mind, one he was sure would take his offer into full acceptance upon hearing of his heroic aid to the dashing Earl of Windhaven. James scowled at him using his urgency as a jest to heighten his friend but he'd deal with that later, after he found his wife.

"I'm sure Lady Lydia would be more than happy to distract you, if you feel too overwhelmed." Clearwater couldn't help but chuckle.

James tightened. "No."

He had dragged Lydia with him to find Eleanor. After that night at her townhouse in London, he knew she was involved somehow. While she didn't have the power, money, or connections to actually plan this abduction, she had other methods. The fact that during their overly heated debate, she tried to seduce him to throw him off the mark only infuriated him more. And when she was rejected, she sputtered, "He said he wouldn't harm her!"

It took James a minute or two for that information to seep into his troubled mind. The master behind this elaborate abduction required information in exchange for promises. While he didn't know what Lydia's portion was to be, she was implicated enough to be here, with him, and sailing West.

Clearwater wiped his forehead with his cuff, dampening the already stained ruffled material, the lace edge the darkest area of all.

"Hotter than hell," he muttered. "Wish for us to make it to the islands Godspeed, too."

James stifled a chuckle. It would do no good to tease the man since he still dressed as if in London and not the seas heading southwest. He, on the other hand, had adapted to the change in dress, wearing nothing more than his linen shirt loosely tucked into trousers, minus the waistcoat, and left his linen jacket in his cabin. It was warm but the ocean breeze drifted through his shirt and cooled him. The fact that it was a simple shirt, not the fancy ruffled lace cuff concoction Clearwater adorned, helped as well. He rolled his sleeves to get down to business of the ship's route and all signs he hoped he could find of Eleanor.

Clearwater guffawed. "Looking like a commoner has you ill-faced by the sun, I see."

"Perhaps. Makes it cooler, that is a fact." He frowned. "I do appreciate your honor to stand with me through this, yet I fail to understand the reason. I know you've spoken of a lady willing to have you but to come on such a long trip when it is not a pleasant experience for you escapes me."

This time, Clearwater laughed. It was a light sound and reminded James of the days before wives were a requirement, back to the time of school. They, plus George, were quite the threesome, constantly hounded by the matchmakers as up and coming lords. The fact that James knew they were more appealing to the eye pushed those lionesses harder to secure them. Through wit and jest, they had evaded the net, and laughed their way at doing so. Clearwater still looked no older than twenty, even though that mark was passed for the sixth time this spring. But his presence was still a mystery of sorts.

"Who else to help keep Lady Lydia at bay? And to help see the fair Lady Eleanor's smile brighten the skies again?"

Youth and money and adventure. James nodded. "My gratitude."

The lady in question came out on the deck, her white dress glowed in the sunlight. She could have been an angel, the hat on her head with a broad brim taking on a halo appearance. He couldn't help but imagine how her horns remained hidden under the crown. She unfurled her fan and waved it madly to break the heat. James blood still curdled at the thought of her being involved in this.

She turned and found him. Her eyes were smoldering with flames, not of desire but of sheer anger. He couldn't help but relish in it for just a moment. In reply, he smiled and gave a tilted nod to her. Despite the sound of the waves hitting the boat and the men moving about doing their chores, James could've sworn he heard her grunt in dismay and stomped off the deck.

It may be only momentary, but James would take it as a triumph in this race against time.

Chapter Fifteen

NIGHT CAME WAY TOO EARLY. It made the lone-
liness way too encompassing, despite every method
James could think of to stop it. He probably didn't help
it any, holding his only portrait of Eleanor, a small gilded
pocket frame piece, encased in leather. He unsnapped the
lock and opened it, red velvet on one side and Eleanor on
the other. As he rubbed the portrait, he wondered how
long the paint would last under his stroking the piece.
The mere thought of losing his only image of her made
him sit back and pinch the bridge of his nose, his eyes
shut tight as the hole in his chest ached at the loss of her
His other hand brought the glass of brandy to his mouth
and he downed the entire contents in one gulp. The burn
brought him back to now but once it hit his stomach, he
deflated.

Where was she? He prayed to God constantly that those
two unhappy pirates were right, that the "witch" with the
sable colored hair was still on this ship, the *Equuleus*, and
heading to the West Indies. The fact that he learned she
was alive and apparently well had sent his heart soaring,

but when he found she was on a pirate ship and in the clutches of Captain Cavendish, his fear for her life spiked. The two drunken pirates only said that Cavendish was not after gold and riches, but revenge for the death of his wife.

Left to her own devices, Eleanor could sway the man to see his errors of holding her, for surely she had nothing to do with that death, and return her to England. But what if she couldn't? What if something had happened to her, being under a pirate's rule? His thoughts and emotions wrapped around him, making him see ghosts of a future without her, of her own death at the hands of this outlaw or by a the sea. What if he sold her to the Barbary pirates? He'd pay whatever sum the man wanted for her return. Anything.

He heard the creak of the cabin door open but he didn't have to look to see who it was. The quiet that followed, the sound of rustling silk loudly announced who it was— Lydia.

She came to where he sat, a short distance from the doorway.

"James—"

"My lord will do." He was in no mood for her.

"Tsk." Lydia swept around the room with her skirt brushing every ounce of the cabin. She swung around to stand behind him, her hands caressing his shoulders. "You are full of knots."

He struggled not to launch off the chair, repulsed by her touch though her fingers did press on the sore spots that begged for rubbing.

"Lydia, what are you doing?"

She pushed harder on his shoulder blade and his body shivered at the kneading.

"I'm trying to get you to notice me."

"You have never been unnoticeable." Two years ago, he found himself under her spell. Long before Eleanor.

She turned around the table to give him a sultry look. "Do you like what you see?"

He exhaled the breath he didn't know he'd been holding. "Lydia, perhaps you should try to keep your innocence."

"What innocence?" She hissed. "You forced me to join you on this voyage to nowhere, to chase a ghost of a ship, in hope of finding her?" She leaned on table, her fists on the table top. "You've ruined my reputation! The least you could do is take advantage of me!"

Her words stopped him. After all this, him interrupting her evening, averting her presence in his bedroom, and his confronting her about his wife's disappearance, he could not believe she came here, expecting to join him in bed. A quick glance, though, showed him she meant business because she closed his cabin door upon entry. Her dress was simple, no wraps, no adornments, and her toes curled under her skirts when he took a glance below. The hair on his neck bristled.

"Miss St. Martin, or more correctly, Lady Wattsmore, as I recall your married name, I believe you have never cared much as to your reputation nor your virtue," he stated plainly.

"How dare you!" She flushed with anger. Years ago, he would have enjoyed how that brought her so alive, so vibrant but now, he just shook his head.

"Frankly, my dear, I'd suggest you explain who is involved with taking my Eleanor." The words were steady, cold, and laced with anger. At least she had the decency to notice that.

"I've nothing else to help with."

Liar. "Tell me what your father has tied up in this." He wanted to know.

She stepped back. "I have no idea what you mean." At his narrowed glare, she fidgeted, her gaze falling and bit her lower lip. "I truly have little clue. I only overheard idle gossip, nothing of important."

In a split second, he thought she was going to expose the truth but, as usual, she hid in vacant words. He snarled. It was loud enough, she jumped.

"Truly, James. Everyone knows the roads in and out of the city are but prime targets for the criminals and vagrants. Words from servants and drunken noblemen are also worth less than a shilling in truth."

He vaulted forward, pulling her into him, his grip tight and he dug his fingers into her upper arms. Still hiding behind a shroud of nothing, Lydia would continue this without his bringing her to line and he only know of one way to change her tune. He bent forward, the words forming a harsh whisper in her ear, "You want me, Lydia? Want to feel me, deep inside you? Then I need the truth."

He heard the muffled mewl escape from her mouth but no words and inwardly shook his head. "Does your virtue mean that little to you?"

Her backbone stiffened. "At one time, you didn't care."

That comment made his right eyebrow raise. The pause stilled the air. "Perhaps, little dove." He inhaled her fragrance. Even at sea, the faint scent of sweet lilacs cloaked her wickedness. He gritted his teeth, suppressing the anger he wanted to unleash on her.

Quickly, he stepped back—not an easy task to do in a room that offered not more than a bed and narrow table and chair, yet he had to as memories of Eleanor crowded his thoughts.

Lydia was a beautiful woman, curved in all the right places to mold in the crux of a man's body. Her ivory skin, covered from the sun even here on this ship, gave her a perfect model for the ton. She was desire and dangerous. It only fueled his irritability.

She spun, facing him with a knowing smile on her lips. "So what do you think? Shall we renew our memories?"

James shook his head. "I am a married man. I will find Eleanor and, despite your keen desire to make our situation more to your liking, I will remind you that we will not revisit that now. You may have thrown your virtue away to other men of the ton, but I refuse to join that brotherhood."

He could see it in her eyes that his denial infuriated her. "She won't return to you, of that I am certain. Then we shall see how you fare." With a toss of her head in indignation, she stormed passed him and out of the cabin, leaving him so abruptly that it took him a moment to breathe.

Anger and fear wrestled for control. She was a tempest, a storm ready to wreak havoc. He knew that before he took her on this trip but he made her board anyhow. It wasn't because he desired her, not now, despite the short wave of it that raced through him a moment ago. No, he needed her to deal with the power behind this abduction. He was sure she knew more than she admitted.

When she stormed off, she left his cabin door open. He took a step to slam it shut, angry that she had the nerve to try to seduce him, when he caught a glance of her under the quarter moon light walking right into an embrace with a man. He focused, trying to discern who it was, because this man might be an accomplice in the kidnapping, which would enrage in further that the asshole was on the ship. The ship had mostly her father's, Lord Attlewood's, crew aboard, so James wasn't sure he'd recognize the man but … something about the two made his brow twitch.

It was a couple in intimate embrace. The sky was too

dark, clouds covering the stars, added with her blocking part of the view, James couldn't discern who the man was. Agitated and too tired to push further, as the man was here with them on this voyage, James shut the door with force and stumbled back to bed and get lost in a dream about Eleanor.

∞

CROSSING THE ATLANTIC SHOULD HAVE been long and arduous. The sun beating down on the ship, the deck a virtual stove top in heat. The dull days of open sea and no land or boats around, the monotony of chores going on around her but her with nothing to do and limited choice of food. But Elle did not find it so. Instead, what she found was a man, rugged, fierce and in charge of the sailors around him. But while Captain Cavendish ruled with determination that pulled the crew together, for her, he was playful, a contrast though it fit him well.

Even now, it was late afternoon, the heat of the day refusing to fade, she sat on the barrel, mending a shirt. Her fingers worked the needle and thread but her gaze often wandered to across the deck to find him returning her look. A smile hinting at his lips. He looked strong, vibrant and alive and alluring, his soul seemed to be calling to her, to her inner core wanted to answer.

"Feelin' your sea legs, missy?"

Not taking her eyes off the captain, she couldn't help but smile at the sound of Fitzgibbons' question. The first officer always checked on her and she became more comfortable to his presence, even looked forward to it.

"Yes, sir," she replied. "In fact, I wasn't aware it was moving."

The Irishman laughed. "Aye, lassie, that's tha way it rolls."

He was behind her. She smiled broadly, finally tearing

her gaze of the handsome rogue on the top deck as she turned to face the seaman. "Why is it I feel as though you're a mischief maker?"

His face contorted in denial. "Nev'r, my lady." But the twinkle in his eyes told otherwise.

She snorted. "It's been peaceful."

The amused look on his face disappeared. "Aye, and tha crew's itchin' fer a prize. They donna do well wit dull."

She frowned, her teeth grinding. "They wish to steal again?" After all, that was what piracy was.

Fitzgibbons looked down, shuffling on his feet. The truth was painfully obvious, but to mouth the words would take away the humorous air between them so she gathered he took a moment of silence to show his meaning and she couldn't blame him.

She lifted her shoulders, righting her stance, her chin also slightly raised. "So why aren't they seeking a prize?"

The Irishman gave her a half-smile. "Surely, ya could take it as to tha reason. You, my girl. You."

Many reasons popped up in her mind, like supplies, not enough ammunition, but her? The thought rolled in her mind as the pirate continued.

"Tha men have noticed how tha capt'n is favorin' you, ta the point of nev'r lookin' tha horizon for prey." He shrugged. "I might be thinkin' he's veered from his fateful death, on tha path he'd been on, thanks ta you. But the men, theys be thinkin' otherwise. Perhaps a curse, bein' a woman here, or that you've conjured a spell on him…"

"Witch?" She shivered at the thought. Casting an indiscreet gaze about the deck, she spied pirates doing their chores. Sailors were a suspicious lot, even Cavendish hinted at that. She hoped with her aid in finding the lost treasure, the label of witch or bad luck, had vanished. Another icy jolt raced down her spine.

"I am neither bad luck nor a witch," she hissed lowly, to not draw too much more notice.

"Aye, that I believe, but they've no loyalty to me." He cocked his head to the side. "Perhaps you might be speakin' to tha capt'n about this, see if he won't change his views." He bent closer. "Men often take a woman's word to heart, after tha heat of takin', if'n you get my view."

The implication hit her like a torch to her stomach as the heat inside blossom and the heat rose to her cheeks. "That goes too far," she managed to voice, her tone steady despite the skip in her heartbeat.

"Ah, lass, they know he's been sleepin' in his lair, where you reside."

Fighting desperately to not show how she felt, for that was a quagmire of emotions, she gave him a faint smile. "This is an inappropriate subject." Inside, she tried to find a way to understand and the message was clear. Trent did sleep in the cabin with her. It was a convenient arrangement. After the rum-soaked afternoon on that island two weeks ago, with that kiss that she relived daily in her mind, they avoided contact with each other except for bed. Well, they fell asleep in each other's arms but with no physical contact outside that, not even a kiss. Nothing that gave her a hint he wanted more. It was as if she was fire when he kissed her and the burn kept him from pushing for more.

"It is his cabin, after all," she continued, her hands busy flattening her trousers like she used to do to her skirts. "The notion is only to protect me from miscreants."

The Irishman laughed. "This is ship more than a boat of miscreants, my lady. Apologies for me pryin'. But perhaps, if ya hinted a raid might be most beneficial..." He raised his eyebrow at her in a questioning manner.

The skin on her neck prickled, giving her a chill even

though it was hot out in the sun. The whole conversation, while apparently one the first mate needed to have with her, was terrible, too invasive, and, in polite society, rude.

But this wasn't polite society. It was a pirate ship. She gulped.

"I guess you are correct." She straightened. This was a pirate ship, where men raided ships to steal the cargo, wielding swords and firing pistols to gain their riches. She was to influence him to plan an attack.

She gave Fitzgibbons a nervous smile, wondering how.

Chapter Sixteen

TRENT LEANED BACK AGAINST THE railing and
closed his eyes briefly. It'd been a long day, most of
it spent on the upper deck, looking at maps and seeing
nothing, or viewing the ocean front but not focusing.
What was wrong with him?

He knew exactly what was wrong with him. Elle. Ever
since that afternoon on the beach, when he allowed himself the simple comfort of another soul, he was lost. He'd
swore there would be no one else besides Rachel. It was
an oath he'd sworn after her death. But now, he was on
shaky territory. So to get some relief, he stationed himself
at the helm to watch over his ship—one that could func-
tion well even without him and that irked him.

The sun was setting on the horizon and with the deck
now awash in pinks and orange hues, he took a deep
breath and realized how starved he was. He ambled down
the stairs to the main deck, stopped by the galley where all
were feasting but found it vacant of Elle. He downed the
spoonful of stew that tasted awful, a taste that didn't surprise him with them being out at sea for almost a month

since the island. But still, he couldn't help but frown and mutter to his first mate of her absence.

Fitzgibbons chuckled. "She's been and gone, Capt'n. You'll be seein' her right directly, I s'pose."

Trent glared at the man but nodded none the less. He shoved the end of the piece of bread down his throat, chased it with a mug of rum, and stood. "To the 'morrow, gentlemen." He parted for his cabin.

The cabin door was slightly ajar, the only light coming from the moon that shined brightly against the clear sky. Slowly, he entered, and upon seeing her curled on the bed, asleep, he moved quietly not to wake her.

Every night, since Fitzgibbons had pointed out to him that she needed his protection, Trent slept in the cabin. At first, he tried to slug it out in the chair but straight back slatted chairs were extremely uncomfortable. The flooring hadn't been any better. The lack of sleep and the stirrings from his groin during those nights made him a grumpy commander the following day. But after their rum encounter, he moved to the bed with her, fully clothed and on top of the sheet. It took several minutes, well, maybe hours, if he recalled correctly, to calm down the stiff rod that wanted to be inside her and sleep, but he had.

As quietly as he could, he unlatched his leather belt clasp and laid it on the desk. Next he slipped off his boots, stockings, and jacket. Standing in his breeches and linen shirt, he stepped to the bed and slowly lowered himself on the goose-feathered mattress, hoping not to wake her. It was a ritual he did nightly, for it would be ill of him to wake her and he feared if she did, he might not be able to stop himself from taking her into his arms and sink deep inside her. Memories of Rachel had kept his libido at bay but a temptress stirring might bury the thoughts of his wife.

He settled in, listening to the sound of the ocean that came through the open porthole. The gentle rocking of the boat eased his tired body and battered soul but the scent of the woman next to him invaded, calling forth urges he thought were dead, or at least hidden. It would be another night of fighting to control his desires. He could win, simply by getting out of the bed, but there was this warmth and need to be with her. He often argued with himself that he probably was the only one with the cravings. She had returned his kiss with ardor at that encounter but her memory still remained vacant. And when it came rushing back, did he want to know the woman he sought pleasure with was married to another man? He was many things—a pirate, a thief, a murderer without a doubt, but not an adulterer. His conscious threw the brakes on that.

Elle sighed softly and turned to face him. He held his breath, waiting for her to resume sleep. The moonlight bathed the room in a glow that he could see her clearly. He knew she often collapsed in one of his shirts but tonight, he saw bare neckline and shoulders. Through the sheet, he detected she had nothing on as she molded against him, the apex of her thighs at the bulge in his groin. Instantly, his mouth went dry and he froze. She snuggled against him. The brush against his cock nearly undid him. But she was asleep…wasn't she?

"It's about time you got to bed," she whispered, her voice husky and dark.

"You should be asleep."

"Yes, that is true, but I was waiting for you." Gently, she reached over and kissed him on the lips. "You taste like rum." She giggled.

The sound rippled through him. It was sensual and enticing. As if she was inviting him to make the next step.

But what if he was wrong.

"You do not want this," he replied, hoping he was mistaken.

She looked at him. Her eyes were dark. He was lost.

"Is that truly what you think?" She kissed him again. "We both have played this farce, that this was comfortable, but I know from part of you that it isn't."

She was right. "You know as well as I that there is more to this than simple pleasure. What if you're a virgin? Or married? And I owe to Rachel…"

"This argument won't work," she murmured, moving to put her leg on his hip.

"Elle…"

Still near him, she reached down to the tail of his shirt and began to raise it. "While my memory fails to return, I feel fairly certain my virtue is no longer an issue. As to marriage, if I was so, wouldn't that feeling return? Is he trying to find me but failed? Or he is the man I ran from." He allowed her to pull the shirt up to his shoulders and he shrugged the garment off. She smiled. And with it gone, she flattened her hand on his chest and slowly traced over his muscles, vaguely aware her hand wandered lower.

"As to Rachel," she continued. "No disrespect, but the woman is in heaven. Surely she would not want her husband to be alone."

His heart thudded loudly, his blood racing through his veins. When her fingers began to work the bindings on his trousers, he could barely think. Memories of a wife long lost didn't pop up, interfering this time. His cock was throbbing, painfully so.

Finally, he muttered, "You would be correct." Then he hissed as she sank her hand into his pants and wrapped it around his hardened member.

In one swift move, he maneuvered the pants off and

threw the sheet into the pile on the floor. He found his answer—she had nothing on. It had been way too long since he'd enjoyed the carnal pleasures of intimacy and he devoured the sight before him. Elle was beautiful. He'd known that from the start. And it wasn't as if he hadn't had glimpses of what appeal her body possessed. But to see it finally unveiled took his breath away. Her skin was ivory with her face, neck, arms, shins and feet sun-kissed. Tentatively, he touched her neckline and let his fingers slowly skim down her, stopping to cup a breast, which fit firmly in his palm. The nipple had pearled and begged him to kiss it. He obliged and scraped it with his teeth. She mewled as her hand slipped to his swollen member and she began to stroke him. Each move made him want to take her immediately, so he removed her hand, allowing him to move freely over her. She started to argue she wanted to continue pleasing him but he hushed her.

"We have all night," he whispered huskily.

He traced over her flat belly, one that was taut, not like the ladies he had had pleasure to know before Rachel. No doubt some work on the ship, despite his telling her she didn't have to, aided in this. His fingers feathered over her hip, round and enticing. But as he exploration turned inward, she gave a mini thrust to her hips.

"Ah, so you are eager to ride the waves," he grinned. "We should stop this…"

She bit her bottom lip, letting it roll out of her teeth. He growled right has his reached for her mound. As he slipped his finger between the folds of her flesh, he found her wet and her lower lips swollen. Another finger slid into her soaking core, the reply was her fingers tightening around the hood to his cock, her thumb stroking over the slit in the head. A pearl drop of his seed answered her.

They were both panting. The temperature in the cabin

had turned hotter. One thing was for sure. If she kept stroking his cock, he would explode, drenching them both. The next one nearly hit that point, enough that he pulled his own hand up to grab hers, shoving it and her other one above her head, pinning her to her back on the bed. In one quick move, he was between her thighs and drove his hardened member home, deep inside her. Her moan to him sliding in her slick sheath was the response he wanted.

United, they slowly began to move in the ancient art of love making. It was sensual, taking him to new heights. The pressure inside him built but he held back. She matched his thrust with her own, meeting him as he plunged harder inside her. What surprised him was she watched him, moaning, her facial features contorting as if she was close but not there yet. In that moment, he released her hands, grasped her rounded hips, and flipped them so she was on top of him. She laughed before a groan took over.

Their love dance picked up momentum. They played the game well and their thrusts multiplied, her sheath tightening every time he entered, coaxing him to release. Suddenly, she shattered, her body pulling him in deep and in seconds, his seed exploded into her as her core tightened hard around him.

Time suspended, both panting, both with an intent gaze on the other. Finally, she collapsed on top of him and he rolled to lay her next to him and he threw the sheet over them.

"Better?" He murmured into her ear.

He could see her grin as she settled back into his arms. "Of course."

"Well, you were right. You were not a virgin."

She turned toward him, puzzled. "And that annoyed you?"

"On the contrary, no." He kissed her lightly. "Makes me hungry for you more."

Frankly, he was surprised that he felt this good and not as if he betrayed Rachel. He paused, wondering. Was he over mourning her? He didn't think so but with Elle here, perhaps he had.

ELLE BASKED IN THE AFTERWARDS of making love to Trent. It was truly beautiful, breathtaking, even. He carried himself in a way that made her wonder if he truly wasn't a lord in disguise. That made her giggle but she held it in, because that thought brought forth a myriad of images she couldn't see clearly. One image was of a couple, her perhaps as one of them? The couple were wrapped in each other's arms and appeared in love. The thought made her heart skip a beat, but her head? Despite her strongest effort to decipher the image, the door to her past remained closed.

She shut her eyes and tried to block the wave of emotions that washed over her. It didn't make any sense. Love, honor, betrayal, freedom... While making love with him was everything she hoped for, there was an urgent sense of it being wrong. Good and bad all wrapped up in one. Her temple began to throb, like it used to. She hadn't really noticed it had stopped plaguing her until now when it returned with a vengeful force. Confused, she gritted her teeth and made herself think of now and how the pirates on this ship were uncomfortable without action, without a prize, and how they blamed her for that. To them, she cast a spell on their captain. The idea of burning at the stake as a witch or being thrown overboard, drove her past the pain. Concentrating hard, she forced herself to return to what she needed to do to survive, and burying the thought that seduction to get him to move forward could be seen as magic. She swallowed.

He kissed her neck, goosebumps raced down her arms. How could she want him but not want him?

"Captain…"

"Perhaps you should call me Trent," he nuzzle into her neck. "It seems appropriate, after all."

"Of course. Trent." She shivered as he returned to kissing her. Warmth built again inside her and she needed to stop it. She fidgeted in his arms, hoping to get his attention off her. "Please. There is something we need to discuss."

He glanced up from laving kisses in the valley between her breasts. "My, that sounds severe, my dear."

"It is."

With a bit of a frown for having his meal interrupted, he pulled himself up beside her. "Continue."

She swallowed. "I've been on this ship for several weeks." At his nod, she went on. "The authorities would now register this boat as a pirate ship, would you not agree?" She didn't pause long. "As so, that would make all aboard a pirate, including me."

He frowned. "I don't believe so."

"Have I not been here during that raid? Did I not keep your goods from being re-stolen by those two vermin?" She watched the flicker in his eyes as he listened in silence. "And if this ship was caught by the Royal Navy, would I not also be prosecuted as a pirate?"

His furrowed brows tightened further. "I don't necessarily agree that you are on the account. You've not signed on to the ship though, if the crew despised you and they wanted to truly rid themselves of you, they could implicate that you were part of them, yet they hold no animosity toward you. Though I can see where your views could be taken. What would you like done to correct this? I tried to return you to London, but if you recall, you adamantly convinced me not to."

She gripped her hands, rustling her fingers and palms, searching for the words. "Then teach me to use a sword."

"A sword?"

Finally, she gave him a genuine smile. The discussion was heading the way she wanted. "Well, I need to learn to defend myself..." she paused. "When the men make me take a step off the railing to the depths below."

"What?"

"They blame me for you not looking for a prize. In fact, some believe I've cast a spell on you." The thought still made ice freeze down her back.

He reached up and kissed her bare shoulder. "Never. They'd have to get through me."

That made her feel better but, she needed him to go further. "That sounds wonderful," she sighed. "But as a captain, you can't be my personal guard." She leaned back into him. "I still want to learn how to defend myself, especially when you find your next raid, which, I'm sure, will be very soon." She turned and kissed his lips lightly.

"Teaching you to use a sword—"

"Is a necessity," she completed. "Because I've heard grumblings below, of restlessness." She stopped, hoping he'd read the need for another capture without actually saying it.

Trent sat upright and glanced out the portal. "Yes, I know the men are hungry. The passage is too dull for them." He gave a slight smile. "And I admit, too much for me, as well." He ran his fingers through his hair. "Damn!"

"Is there nothing to amuse them?" Not that she thought attacking an innocent ship and its crew as an entertaining event but her own fear began to invade the edges of her thoughts. Vague images of the men who haunted her dreams, of the race to escape them, began to cloud her thoughts. Her heart took to beating faster. The notion to run wanted to take control but on a ship out in the middle of the ocean, where was she to run? She clenched her hands into the bed sheets.

He sighed. "It's settled. We'll reach our destination within the next fortnight, if I've figured the time right. I know the shipping lanes. There will be treasures to pursue."

Decision made, he leapt out of bed and with a determined force, to redress. She laid there, watching him. The man was sculpted like the statues of old, the ones of nude males she'd seen with muscles well-defined, moving fluidly. She couldn't help but enjoy, her lips curling, ignoring the burning question in the back of her head as to where she'd seen such statues, for fear the answer might ruin her the pleasure she just enjoyed.

Chapter Seventeen

CLASH! THE WOOD SMASHED FLAT.

"Again!"

Trent heard the pirate's order and grinned as the wooden sticks slashed again. She wanted to learn. He tried really hard not to watch her, but that was impossible. Tory, the radical Frenchman they picked up in Brussels, the one who ignored his countrymen in the current battles for a sail to fortune, was a master swordsman and trained the men when times allowed, like long boating trips. For this, he was easy to convince to train her, but considering Trent knew Tory was an aggressive fighter, he demanded lessons start with wooden slats. Steel only to be used once she was ready. Well, once Trent believed she was steady enough, which might never happen…

"Ya teachin' the girl how ta be a pirate?"

Trent snorted. Fitzgibbons was a nosey first mate. And his closest friend, as close as any pirate could be. The world of pirates did not equate to that of proper society, but then, when had he ever fit in to either? Even his short time in the navy questioned his tolerance of obeying rules… He focused on the maps below him, pulling his scope closer to scan to horizon.

"She wanted to learn and it was a wise suggestion. You know how raids can get out of hand." He paused. "I would not let her be used as a tool against us nor injured in an attack."

"O' course."

He glared at the man. "Do not push me."

"Aye, aye, Capt'n." Fitzgibbons stood quiet for a moment before he added, "But you thought her good enough to let her aboard that prize, true sword in hands?"

Trent gritted his jaw. In an attempt to settle the growing unrest, he found a clipper flying Spanish colors on the horizon. It had been a diplomat's ship, the type that was an easy haul and usually had either the dignitary's wife or mistress aboard, meaning jewels and other riches. Enough to appease the men for a bit. The ship was off a way and while he'd said nothing to the crew, many of them had seen the ship. The mood was already lightening around the deck as they quickly did their chores to be able to clean their weapons for a raid. Elle, of course, was thrilled and brandished her sword as if to be part of the raid, having trained daily for the last few weeks, but despite her growing skill, he still feared her safety during a raid, though she was right. The emotions here among the men had been building against her and him for 'being under her spell.' Pirates, he grumbled.

"That ship held no harm. That captain was a weasel, easy to control, and his men stood down."

"But allowin' her that chance ta stand wit us condemns her ta the account," Fitzgibbons argued.

Damn, of course he knew the man was right! He cussed inwardly. He tried every way he could to convince her to stay inside the cabin, not be seen but this lady had a mind of her own. He doubted if even he'd tied her down, she would've been safe. Yet, there was another monster here, than just her inability to follow orders for safety sake. It was him. He held pride in what she'd accomplished and her forward, break the rules way. Of course, it damned him and put her in death's doorway along with the rest of them. It was a fear and admiration he could not control yet.

"Despite her lookin' mighty fine wit a sword in her fist. May even git use ta her hair bein' all short." The Irishman shrugged.

Trent himself couldn't help but laugh. She jumped off the plank that connected the two ships. The defeated vessel's captain was held in chains, his crew kneeling in the hold, awaiting for Trent's pirates to take everything and either kill them or leave them. It wasn't his policy to destroy the conquered ship nor shore their crew like some pirates did, but he also didn't like pursuit by a captain who discovered his balls after they left. Therefore he often disabled the ship in a manner they could fix, giving time and him the escape.

But Elle wanted a taste of the victory. He didn't want her over but he couldn't deny her either, especially when she found the guts to make the cross-over without his approval. She jumped off, the heel of her large boots making noise when she hit the deck. Wearing brown pants that were too big, an oversized shirt with a jacket also too large, her sex wasn't easy to detect, more so with the large brimmed hat she jammed on her head that clouded her stunning sapphire eyes. Trent, though, did catch something amiss—there were no hints of the long honey brown hair she'd had that even peeked under a hat when she piled it on top of her head. Throughout her time on the Spanish ship, she remained quiet for the most part and left the hat on. But upon return, he scooped her up into his arms, thrilled that the campaign on this ship brought ample rewards of wealth and release for his men.

Her hat fell to the floor. Immediately, he raised her to meet their lips, his right hand moving up her back to the nap of her neck to get to her mane when it hit him how the golden brown hair that had poured out, released from the hat, did not fall down her back. He stopped and looked at her with a frown.

What he found was her hair shorn off at about the mid-neckline. Puzzled, he gave her a questioning look. She laughed.

"It was too long to keep hidden under a hat. Shorter is easier and maybe makes me look less of a threat of being a woman."

"Ahem," Fitzgibbons snorted, instantly dissolving Trent's memory of last evening. He shot Trent a scowl.

"What would you have me do? I won't let her be hurt nor will I discourage her, mainly because I've got a ship to run, not play lady-in-waiting for a one with no memory, thus lacking the good manners to return home." The last he realized he spat out harsher than he needed to. Perhaps he feared the return of her memory now. Because what if she remembered and couldn't get away from him fast enough for a family or husband? He jabbed the map on the tabletop with his knife that had been a paperweight.

"So she'll hang wit the rest o' us by the Crown?" He grunted angrily.

"Fitz…" Trent started, knowing exactly what was driving the man's hostility. He understood it because it rankled on the level as his. "I'll do my best to discourage her."

"Perhaps, laddie, whatcha needs ta be doin' is droppin' her by legit bay or marry her, leave the vengeance as done."

With scope in hand, Trent chose to ignore the first mate. Rachel's soul demanded retribution for her fate. As to his martial status, that was not a topic to be broached, and the man knew that. Still fuming, Trent stared across the sea. The sound of steel clashing now replaced the wood from the deck below. He tightened at the mere image of her. What he was more afraid of was fear he might fall for her. That fear was worse than her learning sword...

Across the ocean, a black dot appeared. He focused and within a minute, answer came. It was another ship. This time, a merchantman ship. He smiled.

A DROP FELL RIGHT INTO HER eye and it stung mercilessly but she couldn't wipe it away without giving her opponent an opening. One he was working hard to make, too. Yet the heat made this more and more difficult and for the first time she could think of, she was dripping with what men called sweat. For ladies, though, it was glistening. That odd and vacant thought drummed up from somewhere deep inside her, making her want to laugh.

Without notice, the man she practiced with made a twist and attacked her from the left. Her counter strike was effectively stopped and she sank to the deck. With a growl of frustration, she glanced at him.

"My dearest, Miles, I must forfeit. I'm too hot to see clearly." She blinked and this time, had a hand free to wipe her brow. It, too, was a sopping mess. Thankfully, she had thrown her hat to the side before this round, though that let the sun beat on her face, making it redder, she was sure. Perhaps not as burned as a few weeks ago, for the longer she stood out in it, the more color she gained. That ivory skin she had cherished no longer remained untouched except in discreet areas, and it made her giggle. After the pain of the burn, the peeling of her skin, the thin layer of copper remained and she knew that would be frowned upon by the upper class, though she couldn't recall any of them by name.

The burly, short pirate chuckled and lowered his weapon. "Of course, lady." He offered his callused hand for her. With a smile, she took it and stood.

"Your lessons are well taught."

He winked at her. "You chose ta throw your lot in wit the rest o' us. Looked mighty fine on that treasure ship. Makin' us proud."

She blushed. Her short walk across that tenuous plank that stretched the two ships was more a test she put on herself than truly taking a cut in the take. But once across, she couldn't help be feel the staggering effect of arriving on the other side and the roar of the pirates. She realized later that simple move pushed her beyond being a threat to them, but perhaps elevated her status to that of pirate. It was a position she hadn't really planned for but, considering where she was, seemed fit.

Of course, that handsome captain might have influenced her on that. The mere whisper of him made her insides melt. When he kissed her, rational thinking evaporated and all she wanted was him. Well, mostly. The ghosts of her past sometimes interrupted what should be sound sleep after love making. She realized something wasn't right but she couldn't put her hand on what. Their second time, both were hesitant. She was sure his was in deference to his deceased wife. No reason formed itself in her mind as to her own and that irritated her. Whatever it was, she managed to push aside mostly, but it beckoned to her, like a hand reaching out for help...

Staring at the sea, enjoying the breeze brushing her

short hair astray, Elle didn't hear Trent walk up.

"How are our skills today?"

She laughed, enjoying his referring to her training as "their" training. Wasn't there a king who talked in the plural? That odd notion came out of nowhere...

"Much improved, Capt'n, much better," her teacher claimed as he gathered the swords and padded away.

"Were you watching?" She nudged him, fighting hard to not grin but she was too happy not to.

"Aye, lassie, I was." His eyes sparkled, no doubt full of mischief. "I fail to see what ye'll be doin' with all these new skills," he stated, using the lazy tongue of a pirate.

"Oh, to be sure, I'd be wantin' to git wit ye on the next routin'," she returned in her version of pirate lingo.

But the mischief in his eyes vanished and he grabbed her arm. "I'll have no chance taken in regards to you. Despite your improving talent, I will ask you remain out of harm's way."

"Of course I will—"

"No!" He spun her around to stand right in front of him and look out over the sea. "Look to the east. We have another opportunity."

She could see the image, though faint, more like a gray blimp on the ocean line. "Who is that?"

He pulled out the telescope and, once extended, he gave it to her to view. "'Tis a British ship, merchantman. Traveling from England to the West Indies, if I were to wage a bet. A ship that size will have goods on it, enough to get us through the next few months." He turned her toward him, the scope tumbling until he grabbed it. "I do not want you aboard her. Being with us as it stands puts you in precarious situation. I will not have your name or face sullied as pirate, do you understand me?"

She shifted, breathless at the chance ahead and the

means to avoid his path. When he didn't release her, she gazed right into his eyes, locking a hold and stated firmly, "I do hear you. And aye, Capt'n'." She curtsied and broke his hold.

"Elle," he warned, his voice low. "You know the crown hangs pirates. Even women pirates. I should have left you someplace safe. Not on this ship, not on this voyage. Being aboard injures your reputation. You being seen with a sword in hand and on the ship with us will damn you as a pirate. Please," he begged. "Stay away from sight. There's always a chance they might put up a fight. British ships tend to fight back, and while the men here would enjoy a good battle, I don't want you hurt."

She bit her bottom lip. His words were heartfelt, the look on his face sincere in concern. Part of her wanted to yell that she would do what she wanted, a freedom that rang from deep inside her, yet it was tempered by his worry. She swallowed the lump in her throat and cast a gaze out across the sea. The ship was still only a dot but that could quickly change. Slowly, she realized she was nodding, acquiescing to his request with some reluctance. While she never doubted it was dangerous—her memory of the first ship they took with her here remained clear—a part deep inside her grumbled about hiding. She did her best to quiet it but a desire for freedom grew with each second.

That nod triggered him to pull her against him, into his arms. A tremble raced through him, she felt it.

"Thank you, my love," he whispered into her ear, one hand cradling her head as he bent down to kiss her.

The words sank deep into her heart. As his lips touched hers, the word rang about her head – *love*. Was he proclaiming his love for her? Her heart exploded with the idea. And as his tongue invaded her mouth, taking up the dance of old with hers, she settled comfortably in his arms. Yes, she was ready to love him and with that, she returned the kiss hard, demanding, matching him.

Then why did the voice in the back of her head beckon her to whisper he's not the one.

Chapter Eighteen

IT WAS ANOTHER SUNNY, HOT day on the Atlantic. James inhaled the salt air, his heart at rhythm with the sway of the ocean. The sea had called to him earlier in his youth, a time when he was part of the Royal Navy. Even a nobleman's son could have a difficult time at sea, under the commander's whip. But the peace the ocean could give a refuge from a brutal world. The sea was long before Eleanor, when as a young man he needed to be tamed, and when he had had his fill, according to his father, he was yanked home to assume his real position. One that called for title and a wife.

He wondered if there was any irony he now had to pursue his wife via the sea…

"So, do you see any?" Clearwater asked, coming up from behind him. "Ships? Spaniards or pirates or so forth?"

James grimaced. Lost in memories of old—a trip he made often of late and the only one to console him— had made him lax in scanning the ocean for problems. Or catching a glimpse of the ship he chased. Still a fortnight from land of the West Indies, he'd given up hope of spotting the ship she was on out here. He pulled up the telescope and looked. He squinted. In the distance sat a ship, one with markings he couldn't decipher. It was red, white and blue but not matching their British flag nor the Americans.

"What are you looking at that has you so intrigued?"

"It is a ship out there. Can't decipher her colors well."

Clearwater snatched the scope out of his hands. Adjusting it to his eye, he glanced outward. James watched him frown.

"That ship is turning toward us!"

James snatched the scope back and adjusted. His friend was right. She had turned, her sails at full mast, billowing in their direction. Only one thought ran through his mind. Pirates. He couldn't help but smile as he prayed it was the *Equuleus*. Then he caught sight of it. One flag of multi-colors lowering and he'd bet be replaced by a black flag.

Instead of impending doom, for he knew this sloop was not made to outrun a ship like that nor were the sailors any match for pirates, he was sure, but a certain level of comfort eased into his bones. Eleanor, come home to me...

"We need to get out of here!"

James turned to his friend. Clearwater looked panicked, all pale and tugging at his necktie. In fact, he'd never seen his friend this agitated.

"You are correct." He passed Clearwater to the captain of the ship, a younger bloke named Sebastian.

"Captain Sebastian, we're going to have company."

The mouthy sailor had already begun issuing orders to raise all sails and turn the ship. "Ain't got guns to take a ship like that on." He spat. "She fires on us, we be gone."

James took a step back. Even he could tell that ship was

closer. Something deep in his core told him Eleanor was on that ship. It'd been nearly two months, give or take a week as he lost count after a while. It was more like an eternity but he could feel it in his bones she was there. He couldn't help but smile.

ELLE SAT ON THE AFT deck, her toes wiggling as her feet dangled from the crate she sat upon staring over the railing at the distant boat with a certain amount of fear and trepidation swirling inside her. The destruction was terrible if they fired on the prey and the blood of the crossing more so and why she'd never be able to be part of the landing. While improving on the sword, she was far from mastered. No, directly after was good enough—and she'd shut her eyes to see the wounded and bloody deck.

She tilted her head so the sea breeze blew her hair off her face. Awful inconvenience, she decided, to have the shorter wisps that had nothing to hold them back so they constantly seemed to find a way into her eyes.

Stay here. Out of sight. Out of mind was more like it. Her hands gripped the crate edge and pain stabbed at her jawline as her teeth gritted. But did she want to throw her life into piracy? What other opportunities did she have ready? It wasn't until well into this voyage that the nightmares faded. Not entirely gone but the idea of sleep, of closing her eyes to slumber, scared her until recently. Though she wondered if that happened because of sleeping with Trent. She wasn't sure but enjoyed the idea none the less.

"Where are your thoughts, my lady?"

She smiled. Fitzgibbons. "Tell me about that ship?"

He peered over her shoulder. "She be a merchant ship. A nice one, fer sure. No doubt ta carry the man who exceeds at his sales." He snorted.

"So many riches?"

He shot her a look, brows furrowed. "Maybe. From the looks o' her, I'd be guessing yea. Since when did ya turn pirate?"

She laughed though it was somewhat hollow for it was a question she asked herself. Dressed like them, learning to fight with a sword from them, made her question who she was. It might have helped her if she knew her past but at this point, she gave up on that returning to her. Pity...

"Perhaps that is my calling." She smiled. Or a pirate captain is... That mere thought made her tingle. If she could just understand why she couldn't just be overly happy with him. It was annoying to say the least, for the attraction was there, he could make her smile with bed play but there was something that told her he wasn't the one. Why, though, she couldn't decipher.

"There be ladies takin' the account, for sure," Fitzgibbons stated. "But it be a hard one. Always under watch by the crown. You'll swing from the noose, like the rest o' us."

"So is that what Trent fears? The noose? Or the idea of that for me?" The questions just spilled out of her mouth.

Fitzgibbons opened his mouth but the answer came from the man himself.

"I have no fears for myself, nor for this crew." Trent walked up behind her and took her into his embrace, pulling her back into his arms. "You, I do hold them for. It is a hard life, with little reward."

"And that is why you have a ship with a full a compliment of men willing to follow you, all for no gain? Ha!"

He rested his chin on top of her head. "Point well taken. But you are a delicate flower, thrown into a world where nothing is sacred, nothing is safe. I do not want you crushed by it."

A shiver raced down her spine at the notion that he

held her in such regard. "Tell, sir, are you a pirate or a white knight?"

He chuckled. "The first is correct, the latter is one I've never been referred to as. Thief, outlaw, murderer," he listed, the last with a raised tongue, as if he worried she wouldn't like it. "Many times. But I don't want you in the same condition."

She bit her bottom lip. His solemn tone made her fidget, the tension in his arms a contrast to his stance so she turn and looked at across the span of ocean to the other ship. "Then I'll do my best to not be."

He kissed the nape of her neck. "Do not be troubled by such. You stay here, out of sight, and you will not be held accountable of the acts of piracy."

She couldn't help be adore him more. Then he released her, springing into action of issuing orders to his men and the upcoming attack. The fury that was to unleash overwhelmed her and for once, she was glad he was here. He would make it all right, even through the bloodshed. She shivered and left the decking as the cannons rolled into place. Hell was about to explode here.

TRENT CARESSED HER EARLOBE, HIS teeth pulling slightly at the piece of flesh, doing his best to distract her from travelling down the road to her damnation, throwing her lot in with his unholy trade. He was in it to avenge Rachel, not to destroy this sweet angel.

He glanced across the waters at the boat they were pursuing. The sloop flew a British flag. Only wild hopes ran through his mind that Rachel's murderer was aboard but more likely, this ship could be Elle's salvation. The closer they got, the more his plan began to form.

He pulled her back and gave her a deep kiss on the lips,

tasting every part of her and putting it to memory for that maybe the only place to keep her safe. A whirlwind of lilies and cinnamon exploded on his tongue, every flavor a bit of her. Lily the soap he gave her to wash with and cinnamon the spice that she craved.

He'd hate to give her up but this was no life for a lady. The fact that her memory had not returned concerned him. Doc had shrugged, suggesting that life on the sea gave her mind no reference point to trigger its return. It might never return and Doc stated that people can live, restarting fresh, without a past, though it could hit her later and at a point of no return the longer she stayed in the dark world of pirates. That nagged Trent. She was a lady, born and raised, for she carried all the signs of such in her demeanor, the way she walked upright and proud with a sway to her step, even in sailor clothes. Her speech was that of a proper education. So who was missing her back in merry ole England? A family, a husband? He prayed for neither, therefore not be plagued with guilt for keeping her with him. But this was not the life for her. He buried his face in the crook of her neck, the tousled cut hair caressing his cheeks and forehead.

He had no choice. Attack the British ship, damn himself and crew further into piracy, and find a way to get Elle back to London. And for that, earn her hatred. Searing pain stabbed him in the gut like a sword blade as it dawned on him the agony of her departure. The grind to his chest was because he found himself in love with her. Damn!

The *Equuleus* sailed closer to her prey. Over her shoulder, Trent could see the men on that British ship moving. It was time to prepare. With a touch of reluctance, one that was in his bones, he pushed Elle away, and strode purposely to the top deck.

"Aye! She's ours! Set the guns and prime! Davy, bring her to the portside and raise the gun portals!"

The men scurried to follow his orders. The Britisher was theirs. God and saints above, save us all. It was a prayer he always said before an impending attack. But revenge was vacant, replaced by thoughts of conquer and the release of Elle to safety. His heart clenched.

Chapter Nineteen

JAMES GRIPPED THE RAILING BUT ducked as another cannon volley hurled toward the ship, crashing into the railing further down, splinters flying in the air. The decking rumbled at the impact as the vessel rolled on the sea. A scream ignited along with men wailing and yelling, the crew and captain working to keep the *Olympus* from sinking.

Clearwater stumbled beside him. "Quite a show, hey ole man!"

James grimaced. His friend's sense of humor was ill-placed. "Show isn't the phrase I'd use. More like hell, to be exact."

"Aye, true." Another volley had Clearwater latching onto the capstan next to them to keep from falling. A yelp caught their attention as another sailor fell to the decking, blood surging from the open wound in the man's leg, one that left a trail as his fellow mate pulled him to the side. "But you'd have to admit, it is colorful."

"Poor choice of words." James yelled to be heard above the battle.

Despite Captain Sebastian's claim that the *Olympus* did not have the guns to repulse a pirate ship, they were standing their own at the moment against such odds. One that was ill-fated as the other ship loomed closer.

"Can you tell who it is we're trying to stop?" Clearwater pushed.

With the other ship firing the first volley before it got close enough, the smoke filled the air, making it more difficult to find who it was. If he could only make out the pirate ship's name…James grunted, frustration equal to the battle. He shook his head before maneuvering toward the aft, which was closer to the ship's stern. There he'd find the ship's name. If only it was…

There was a lull in the battle as the attacking ship was within range for a spokesman to yell across the expanse, demanding surrender. In that moment of steady decking, James with Clearwater in tow, moved to the end. Withdrawing the scope he'd borrowed, James peered down its tube and barely made out the letters. *Equuleus.* His heart skipped a beat. Eleanor…

"So," his friend muttered as he positioned the scope. "We've found the ship." He turned toward James as another cease fire came, along with the demands. "Not the best of ways, to be sure, as I fear the ever brave Captain Sebastian is giving us up to this pirate who stole Lady Windhaven."

James gritted his teeth. "Sebastian is a puss," he hissed. But a necessary one if this was the ship that Eleanor escaped to.

The slam of wood on wood reverberated the decking as the walking plank hit The *Olympus's* railing. A boarding party, armed to the teeth, crossed. Being at the aft did a lot him prime seat in the spectacle. The few brave sailors threw down their swords as the first of the pirates arrived.

They were a scurrilous lot. Barefoot and in clothes that were an allotment of tattered silk and ruffles, their hair far from fashionable and many wearing rings and ear-rings along with other pieces that James knew the cost far exceeded what any sailor made. With ample ease, they leapt onto the deck, swords at the ready only to be greeted with surrender.

The whole scene rubbed James wrong but he willed himself to remain still.

A tall man, flourished in a faded black frock coat, gray pants, and high-top boots joined the rest. He wore a feathered hat and the brim on it shielded most of his face from James's view, but he could see the man's long brown hair queued with a black silk tie and the gemstone rings adorned his fingers, fingers that were wrapped around the cutlass that gleamed in the sunlight. He strode up to Sebastian.

"Word comes to me that you are the captain."

Sebastian gulped, though his shoulders remained locked. "Aye, I command the *Olympus*."

Even under the shade of his hat's brim, the man smiled. "Excellent."

The conversation faded from James's ears. Not that he cared. He was too busy scanning the other ship for any sign of her. *Eleanor, where are you?*

"Do you see her?" Clearwater's whispered.

James shook his head.

They stood to the side, near the rear of the ship. James tried to place himself not too close to the passage way to the lower decks and hold. No point standing in the way of these vermin, who crossed the distance between the two ships, wielding weapons and smarting looks of victory.

"They're nothing more than pick-pockets," Clearwater added, the disdain in his low tones easily detected.

"Then they're fancy ones at that, carrying those swords the way they do." James also noticed the pistols that were jammed into their waistbands. Resolute in case any of the crew or passengers resisted. A chill raced down his spine to think his beautiful wife was caught up with these villains…

As the pirates scurried about the ship, throwing sneers at the ship's crew as they collected what few weapons the first officer and other high ranking sailors had. Some went below to pillage through the cabins for riches, while others searched those on deck. One wretched scoundrel stalked to James and Clearwater.

The man didn't say a word as he rummaged through Clearwater's frock.

"I dare say!" his friend hissed.

The pirate stopped and gave Clearwater an evil grin. "Aye, 'tis hard fer ye, but bett'r ta let me take while you still be breathin'."

Clearwater's eyes widened and he shut his mouth right as the pirate yanked the ring off his finger. He turned to James, who shot him a hard glare. The pirate righted himself and gave him a quick glance over.

"For dressin' like a nabob, you ain't carrin' much." He spat, taking the only fancy piece James had on him—a lace handkerchief.

James growled, watching the thief head to the next victim. It was the linen Eleanor had given him on their wedding night. Bastard!

Suddenly, there was a high-pitched scream from one of the cabins. James and Clearwater spun toward the cause and James inwardly laughed.

"Poor sot," Clearwater murmured, still rubbing his naked fingers. "Only Lydia would argue with a pirate."

It made James smile but it lasted only a second. Behind

him, light footsteps on the crossing plank caught his attention. He shut his eyes and prayed for a moment then turned. The answer to his chase stood on the plank, tall as she could be. Eleanor. His heart skipped a beat and a smile came to his lips but the sight that it was her abruptly distorted by how she appeared. This was his wife?

"In all that is holy, I can't believe what I'm seeing." Clearwater's surprise laced on each word, words that equaled the same thoughts as James. "She's a bloody pirate?"

Standing tall and proud, Eleanor, the Lady of Windhaven, scanned the deck. The moment of her just there took James breath away. She was dressed in brown trousers that were shoved into the tops of black boots which were way too big for her. The white linen shirt, opened at the neck in, peeked out of the large faded black frock she wore. The straw hat that perched on her head wasn't as large as the pirate captain's but it had a brim to keep the sun off her face. He could see her sparkling blue eyes and sun-kissed cheeks that rose a bit as she smiled that devastatingly adorable grin he loved. And her hair, those long light brown curls he had run his fingers through was chopped to her shoulders and all disarrayed from the wind. In her hands, she too held a short sword. It made her look wild and exotic. A look he devoured like a trifle and demanded more. He was at a loss of words but what he couldn't say, his body did.

Trying to take the vision before him in, of his lady, the woman of his dreams, James breathing stopped. Her eyes had glanced his way and for a moment, however short it was, he hoped she'd see him but she didn't. Instead, her look stopped in the direction right of him, close to the mast where Sebastian stood. He and that leader of the pirates. The scene that unfolded cloudy his thoughts.

His wife, Eleanor, dressed like a pirate, turned her head

toward the pirate captain. James was crushed because it was a deliberate search and when she gave the pirate her lop-sided grin with a wink to her eye, he moved to devastated. James knew that look. It was what she gave him, this coy smile and blink.

James stood, locked in place, his blood boiling, his mind fighting through the confusion and disbelief at what he saw.

"Ah, guess the Lady found another protector." Clearwater shook his head. "Did she see you?"

He really didn't hear him, nor anyone else. The pounding in his ears drowned out most of the surroundings. Why didn't she see him?

His torture ended as the pirate ordered her back to the other ship and she jumped onto the plank and shot him a look over her shoulder, a wink of her eye, and she sauntered back across like a lady...dressed in pirate clothes, sword in hand. He watched, agonized, a knife twisting in his gut.

She'd forgotten him. She'd betrayed him by being with another man. Standing on the deck, feeling as if he were stark naked and vulnerable, he clenched his fists at this side. He needed control. What the hell had happened?

H E COULDN'T DECIDE IF HE was mad at her for disobeying his command to not cross to the captured ship and be thrown in with him and the crew as pirates or if he'd follow her back. Her sashaying hips and that seductive smile she threw at him, looking over her shoulders as she climbed the plank, called to the animal in him. He so wanted to bury himself inside her – damn! It took him a minute to calm the beast within and to cool the flames of anger and lust to be able to return to the business before him. As he watched her reach his ship, he turned his attention back to this spineless captain and the treasure to be found.

What he hadn't expected was the man to the side who gazed at him with hatred written plainly for all to see. Inwardly, he shrugged it off. Wasn't he the one he heard dressed like a nabob but held no riches? He'd picked up the man's scent, as it was, when Elle crossed and jumped into his arms. Not the ideal picture to give to a ship that was captured—he taught his crew well, to never show emotions outside elation of the capture and to never give attention to anyone, for fear the captives could find a use of that to needle a way into their bonds and get free.

But Elle wasn't truly a pirate, despite her appearance and growing mannerism. Nor was she a thief. He'd plan to find her a drop point, though she tugged at his heart more and more each day, which was exactly why he needed to find that point now. Before more damage could be done. Irritated and frustrated, he wheeled on his heel toward his captive and hoped the man could squat miracles.

"The books you seek are in the captain's quarters," Sebastian grounded out. The captain gripped at his side, applying pressure to where he had been wounded.

"The manifest as well?"

At Sebastian's nod, Trent pushed past him to the quarters and within minutes, found the books he needed. A quick perusal gave him the information he wanted and with a grin, closed one of the books, tucked it under his arm and left. On his way topside, he ran into Fitzgibbons.

"Find what your lookin' for?" the first mate asked.

"Twin-fold." He tapped the book in his grasp. "The men?"

"Aye, the hold is about clean'd, the ship's treasures included. Though there is a lady, mos' insistent we be leavin' her bags."

Trent laughed. "Nay."

"Aye, that's what I'd tole to the boy. Ladies can be such wick'd creatures." He spat overboard in the waters below.

"And what of those two over there?" Trent tipped his head toward the back of the ship. "They give all the marks of nobility."

"Aye. Possible ransom?"

Kidnapping added to the rest of his crimes. In the end, it all justified the means, he decided. Because they could be a link to the vile lord who took Rachel...or not, in which case, they'd be cash. He nodded. With his head slightly cocked, he strode casually to them, even letting his boots scuff on the decking. In taking his time, he assessed the two and made a couple quick decisions. He stopped before them and turned to the one on the right, the one who's shoulders tightened and the man gritted his teeth.

"Lord?" he inquired.

The man's gaze narrowed but didn't answer.

Trent raised an eyebrow. "Refusal will do you no good. I have the manifests and your name will be listed."

"Earl of Windhaven."

"Aye, see? Did that truly hurt?" He waited but there was no comment. "Let me extend the hospitality of my ship, the *Equuleus* ." He gave a slight bow as he motioned the ship next to this one.

"What if we decline?"

The man next to him stared, his jaw dropping open with a state of shock on his face. "James," he hissed. He didn't look please, Trent noticed. In fact, this one paled as he studied them.

"My lord?"

"Viscount of Clearwater," Windhaven spat.

"Certainly, Lord Clearwater, perhaps you can persuade

your fellow lord to accept this invitation." He glared at
James as he yelled over his shoulder to Fitzgibbons. "Clear
the decks! Put those not taking the opportunity into the
dingy and burn her!"

"Aye, aye, Capt'n!"

∽∾

"YOU'LL BURN THE SHIP? YOU can't! This is —
Ouch!" Clearwater winced as the other elbowed
him with a hiss. He shot James a glare but James narrowed
his gaze and gave a shake to his head, warning him to be
quiet.

James knew this pirate captain concentrated on him,
trying to decipher the message. Well, he could take that
to hell! Instead, he turned the tables on him. "And who
might you be to destroy property that isn't yours?"

The man straightened and then bowed slightly, in a
flourish. "Captain Cavendish, at your service." He swept
the hat from his head as his knees bent, then he straightened. "My lords, I invite you to join me and my crew on
the *Equuleus*. This ship will no longer be a good vessel for
your journey."

James heard the small gasp from Clearwater, yet that was
all his friend said. Enter the pirate's domain. The promise
of Eleanor was across that wooden beam. Her presence
here puzzled him and it was one he'd unravel as soon
as he could, if he could stay alive to do so. Pirates....he
shook his head. To all the saints, he prayed furiously for
help.

Chapter Twenty

SOMETHING WASN'T RIGHT. SHE COULD feel it in her bones. As the pirates returned to the ship, they carried crates and barrels, talking joyfully on the catch. Among their ranks were some of the sailors from the other ship, not many but a few, their uniforms giving her pause for they didn't act as if captives, more conversing amiably with the pirates. She tilted her head, straining to hear but couldn't.

Also among the group came two men and a woman and they stood out boldly. Dressed in finer cloth, they moved with an elegance, like royalty. They weren't talking nor did they look happy. In fact, the woman wore a scowl. When they hit the deck, two pirates escorted them down into the hold, where the treasures were kept.

Elle frowned. It was a mystery and one that rubbed her wrong. There was something about those people going below that struck a nerve deep inside her, one that beckoned her to follow them. She waited until the deck cleared. She padded across the planks, having kicked her boots off the moment she got back to the *Equuleus*—they pinched the balls of her feet because they were too big. Now she was thankful for bare feet as they helped quiet her approach.

What she discovered sent her heart into her throat. Below the deck, in the cavernous space of the hold, she looked past the hammocks of the crew and at the opposite end, all the treasures stacked away in crates and barrels, to the barred panel. She'd never really went that far in the hold nor cared what was in the back since the area made her queasy with the darkness and vermin that crawled through it. But now she looked and discovered that panel was connected to another to form a cage, one large enough to hold people.

She drowned the gasp that was almost audible when she saw their "guests" inside them, a padded lock on the doors. The woman stood in the corner, arms crossed and anger upon her face. One of the men paced, which was hard to do in the small space. The other one, the dark haired man, sat, almost lounging on the crate in the cell. Her gaze lingered upon him. He was dressed more casually than the other man, with his coat unbuttoned, the waistcoat beneath also undone, the ruffled shirt peeping obviously, and he missed a cravat that the other worn. His brown hair was cut short and clean, unlike Trent's longer locks, and with his square jawline, he had a very masculine, very authoritative look, as if this situation of being held captive, did not phase him. Somehow, her inner soul nodded, as if confirming her assessment of him. Her stomach flipped. Not only did these captives move her, it also struck a nerve. She needed to talk to Trent.

No one seemed to notice her presence, but then again, she hadn't gone far down the steps. So she slowly backtracked, heading back to the deck where she found him, books in hand, heading toward his cabin.

"Captain," she called. He didn't turn. "Trent!"

He dropped the books on the tabletop and snapped. "What?"

"We've gone to taking captives?"

He stared at her. "As I recall, my lady, you are a guest here. Therefore, they are not your captives."

She frowned, confused, deciding to ignore that comment. Bending him around her finger was an option she might be able to use—later. So she chose a different line. "Why are there cages in the hold? Those were not designed for animals."

He sat back in the straight back chair and glared. "They're obviously nobility." He ran fingers through his hair. "Do you recognize them?"

Elle bit her lower lip as she thought hard. "No. Why?"

A moment passed before he answered, in a voice that was colder than she liked. "I had thought that, being a member of that class, you might." He shrugged and returned to his books.

His apparent lack of emotions to the caged people below made her want to stomp her feet. She knew the hold would quickly be hot and stuffy by her own experience. That and the fact that he was ignoring her, concentrating on the books. What was in them that made him bypass everything else, like the treasures below and their captives. She wanted to scream but instead, she threw out, "And those sailors? Or those left?"

"The ones who joined the account are welcomed aboard. The rest will float." He shrugged, which confused her further. "Elle, it is the name of the seas. Another ship will collect them. There are many who sail here, so don't worry."

She twisted her lips, frustrated. He seemed so indifferent…or distracted. What was in those books?

"You'll burn their ship? Isn't that a waste? Why not let them go on it?"

"It is not done. That ship is part of a larger catch. I want it burned." He looked at her and as hard as she tried, she couldn't stop her look of horror—she couldn't close her mouth or keep her brows from rising and her eyes popping wide-open in surprise.

"Burn it?! That's an English ship!" she blurted.

He shot out of the chair and took her hands with his, whispering soothing tones. "Elle, we are at war. Ships sink and burn."

"We are not fighting ourselves!"

He cupped her cheek and brought her closer to where their foreheads touched. In that moment, she realized she was trembling. She steeled herself but couldn't resist the heat of his touch.

"Elle, love, we are. Pirates are constantly hunted by the Royal Navy." He kissed her forehead.

She wasn't sure she wanted his touch. A shiver went down her spine. She inhaled and couldn't get a breath. Her chest hurt, her heart beating frantic, and her ability to breathe turned hard. She needed air, fresh air. Twisting to disengage herself from his embrace, she did notice the books on the table had handwritten titles on them reading the *Equuleus* Manifest, an odd title but it didn't stop her from pulling away. Freed, she nodded and backed out of the door to the deck.

Once outside, she relaxed and inhaled the sea air. Her lungs filled and she settled but mentally, it made no sense. She frowned. Trent wasn't acting normal, nor did she believe he would as long as these nobs were aboard. But why? She looked down and found herself at the foot of the steps to the hold and the mystery below. Puzzled, she toyed with the idea of talking to them. The men and woman intrigued her, but why?

JAMES STOOD, HIS ANGER BUILDING. His heart pounded hard, his thoughts racing through his mind at lightning speed. Eleanor was here, with a pirate. She looked well except she was dressed as a pirate, which was hard to swallow. Perhaps a change of clothes, a weak inner thought queried, but when she threw herself into the arms of the pirate captain, her eyes and smile only for that decrepit man, a wave of surprise, confusion and hate wound around his heart and speared his stomach. What the hell had happened?

Lydia plopped herself back onto the crate with a huff. James broke his clouded thoughts and saw the chit. It was the distraction he needed at the moment because he simply couldn't believe what he'd witnessed above.

"No takes, hey sweet?" he cooed to her.

She shot him a nasty look. "None of these wretches know how to treat a lady!"

He bit back a laugh. She'd tried to coerce her freedom from any pirate that came close to her. Many sidled up to her, just to hear her seductive words but even he knew she'd never give herself to a pirate.

In an attempt to console her, Clearwater sat next to her and offered his shoulder, whispering in her ear that all was well. It made James wonder how he thought he could promise that. His friend had looked sickly when the pirates seized them, a look of fear easily detected in his eyes, but the pirate captain ignored them. The man's interest lay in the bound books taken from the Sebastian's quarters. With just a flip of his head toward them, he'd barked orders for his men to take them to here. Once the man escaped from view, Clearwater's vitality returned, making James wonder. As time marched forward and they were left alone, the inertia made Lydia settled in next to Clearwater and they both fell asleep, James stared. They'd make a great couple. Perhaps that was the only way Lydia could survive...

A shuffle on the floor caught his attention and he spun to find Eleanor standing there, her head tilted with a puzzled look on her face. Joy raced through him. She came to see him! All was not lost. Her short hair caught his attention. He loved her long sable curls to run his fingers through or to grab in his hand as he plowed into her... The look upon her face made him believe those memories were absent. But why had she cut it off? Or had the pirates? His anger returned.

"Good evening, my lady." He spoke softly though the pounding in his ears made him think he was too loud.

She bit her bottom lip absently as she looked him over. "Who are you?"

That was an odd question. "The Earl of Windhaven, at your service." He bowed.

His reply from her was a giggle. Not what he'd expect from his wife.

"Quite a fancy one, hey?" She smiled and his heart melted again. It intrigued him that she didn't go further.

"And?" He prodded her.

A look of confusion, mixed with surprise, flashed in her eyes. "I go by Elle."

Elle? James stood speechless. This was Eleanor, right? The hair color was right, the eyes that same sparkling blue, her height was the same as he recalled, and those lips, pouty and pink, ever so inviting. The clothes hid her shape mostly and the urge to grasp her waist surged through him, for the fit of his hands on that curve was imbedded in his soul. But he stood still, every nerve on fire. Why didn't she come to him?

He tried a different tactic. He smiled. There was a flicker but it was so short, he almost missed it. The lump in his throat turned as big as the rock of Gibraltar.

"How long have you been a pirate?'"

She fidgeted, averting her gaze from his at first. "Not long. Why?"

"Elle!" A voice from the stairs yelled with an Irish lilt.

She shot a glance toward the stairs and gave him another look before turning to leave.

"Don't leave," James begged. She was so close, he could almost feel her, despite the bars. But something wasn't right.

It was if his plea fell on deaf ears for the moment the words parted his lips, she took off at a run for the stairs and disappeared.

Chapter Twenty-One

TRENT CLOSED THE MANIFEST, SAT back in the chair, and smiled. His prey was close. The vengeance he sought was within hand's reach. Bastard took Rachel and he'd pay for it!

At that moment, the cabin door flew open and Elle raced in, slammed the door and breathed deep, trying to catch her breath. Trent watched, waiting for her to talk but nothing came.

"Sweetling, are you all right?"

She nodded than ran straight into his lap, throwing her arms around his neck. "That's what I needed. To feel your arms around me." She bent forward and nuzzled at his neck, her fingers undoing his queue tie in the back.

He chuckled as she started to work on removing his waistcoat, her speed quick, as if she was desperate. "So raiding ships makes you into a seductress? I might grow to fond of that." He paused as she kissed him hard only to return to unclothing him. "Perhaps will drive me further to seek other treasures just so I get this."

She sat on his lap, busily working the buttons and finally

got the last one, throwing the garment over the table where it hit the floor. As she started to undo his shirt, he growled and scooped her up into his arms to take her to bed.

It wasn't the first time she'd taken the lead in bed play but her enthusiasm here outdid any before. Within minutes, they were entangled on the mattress. She kissed him like the world was on fire and frankly, he felt those flames, too. His hand cupped her breast, holding it in place so he could suckle from her nipple. Her response was quick, as she arched her back and a mewl escaped her lips. His hardened cock nudged against her thigh, seeking the moist apex between her legs but he withheld to finish his taste.

The urgency surprised him. What had truly driven her to this demand for him? It was a question that would wait as their bodies joined. She was wet and willing but once he entered her sheath, he knew something wasn't the same. Oh, her body took his cock with ease and the movement of her hips to match his was dead on, but it was off. They went through the motions but it was like she wasn't into it. In fact, did he just witness a tear?

ELLE COULD FEEL HIM FROM the moment they started. No, that she started, she reminded herself. The driving need to be with Trent intimately had her racing to the cabin and on his lap in seconds, like lightning. What had pushed her to this? Was it the raid, like he suggested? Or was it that nobleman? There was something about him that triggered a spark in her. To what end, she didn't know and it scared her. Seeking solace in Trent's arms was the only way to suppress that tug inside her she couldn't explain. But that was a mistake she realized too late.

Trent pulled her close in the aftermath of their lovemaking. "That was a nice surprise," he murmured in her ear.

She twitched at his embrace, as if it wasn't right. Quickly, she hid that response with a smile as she snuggled against him. "I went to see the prisoners." His body tensed behind her. Made her have to steel her own courage to continue. "I went to see how they could be of use, as treasure. They are titled." He nodded. "Ransom?"

He ignored her question. "I thought I told you not to go. The hold is no place for a lady."

She twisted in his arms to face him, a frown on her face. "You often refer to me as lady yet tell me to stay away from the type of people I should have kin with."

Even by the oil lantern's dim light she saw the conflict in his eyes.

"I worry only for your safety, my darling," he whispered and lean forward to pull her back again and kissed her.

She wasn't appeased. "How long are they to remain our guests?"

He rolled away and stood, reaching for his britches. "A week at best. Tides will have us on shore as early as four days if we're lucky."

"You've yet to tell me where we are headed."

Shrugging his shirt on, he added, "Kings Point, Jamaica."

"Isn't that a royal port? Not a good place for pirates." She shivered and pulled the bed sheet up tight.

With a snort, he tied his hair back. "'Tis true, but we are not pirates, now, are we?"

Her eyes opened wide. "You've raided ships, taken goods, even destroyed a British vessel, with captives aboard yet you claim this is not pirating?"

"Elle, now is not the time to argue." He grabbed one of the books off the table. "Stay away from our guests and I'll finish looking at this as soon as I am able." And with that, he strode out the door, making sure to shut it.

"*Grrrr!*" She punched the small pillow and sat there, fuming.

∞

DAWN'S RAYS SLOWLY EKED THROUGH the boat's wooden slats and down the staircase. James had watched its arrival, knowing it meant another day of trying to catch Eleanor's attention, though for the last two days, she hadn't ventured down the stairs once that he knew of.

"James," Clearwater started. "Simply claim her as your wife. It is your right to do so."

He snorted. "And who on this ship would care on legal matters since they don't follow any laws."

"Because this goes beyond English laws," his friend prodded. "You can demand your right by the captain and he'll—"

"If you'll recall correctly, it was said 'captain' who demanded us to be here and locked the door. Somehow I don't think me claiming her will be applauded."

Lydia laughed. "How revealing it is to see how the Lady Windhaven will spread her legs for any pirate."

James bolted off the crate, his anger climbing, and she looked like a good target to let that rage out. But Clearwater's hand slammed into his chest. "James, we're all in a bind here. Lydia is a lady."

"Insulting my wife will not be tolerated!"

"I apologize," she replied, though James wasn't sure of her honesty in that. "I spoke badly."

The urge to still correct her rang through his ears but he didn't. He worked to contain this energy. He ran his fingers through his hair, a habit started early in this search. "How far are we from that island?"

"Nie on two days till we hit Jamaica. I've been here once already this year and recall the landmarks," Clearwater replied. He frowned. "The governor there has strict orders to hang all pirates. Surely you don't think this pirate, what was his name?"

"Cavendish," Lydia whispered, the name rolling off her tongue with a seductive tone.

"Right," Clearwater continued. "You don't think Cavendish would anchor at the beach with the inevitable noose over his head?"

"I'm not sure he won't," James concluded. "He appears to have his own plans."

"How can you be sure?"

"Oh, I can't. But there are ways to find this out and I believe my Eleanor could hold that key, in a manner of speaking." The truth was, he feared she did and how she held that position made him uncomfortable, mad even. Yet he recalled the man's look when he emerged from the cabin, the stack of ledgers in his arm. It was a look of satisfaction. Yet paper and pen held little value for pirates.

"How do you plan to get her back?" Lydia interjected. "You think I am in a bad situation with the ton, what of her? Coercing with pirates, sleeping with them—"

"Lydia," Clearwater warned.

"Well, 'tis truth, as seen by our own eyes." She narrowed her gaze at James. "Will you take her back?"

The girl was irritating, yet her words spoke truth. How could he woo his wife back, particularly from a cage in the hold? He rattled the idea around in his head and then turned to the pirate who just arrived. The man sat, sharpening a blade of a sword. So they now had a guard, James mused.

"Good afternoon," James started. "Can I take a moment of your time?"

❦

ELLE SAT ON THE SIDE of ship, feet dangling over the water below. It was a habit she adopted and found it relaxing. Perhaps she spent too long doing so as the skin on the top of them was a finely tan color, no longer the red burn they had turned in the beginning. The pristine ivory was long gone. They matched her arms, neck and face. Inwardly she moaned. While she didn't mind the color, she wondered just how society would judge her. A laugh escaped her. She sailed with pirates, hardly the experience they possessed. But still, deep inside, a tiny thread remained—how would they treat her? The thought made her nerves chill.

That thought made her twitch. Trent. She found, for a while, comfort in his arms and even now, there was a safety being there.

What she wanted was those English nobs gone because she was convinced they were the ones who interrupted her thoughts.

"Lassie, ya look upset."

Fitzgibbons. She smiled. "Oh, I'm good."

"Uh hum," he murmured, leaning against the railing. "Aye, well," he gazed out across the deck, "tha capt'n'll be bringin' her inta Port Royal."

The land was taking shape in the distance. "But isn't it owned by the Crown?"

The first mate smiled. "Aye." He bent his head down, giving her a knowing look. "And the prisoners ta be released."

As if on cue, there was a commotion in the center of ship, near the stairs to the hold. She'd witnessed this the last three days, where that man, Lord whoever, maneuvered their temporary freedom from below for a chance to come on deck. Being at sea made escape highly unlikely, so the man won that battle. Granted, she agreed, from her exposure to it, it was dark, musty and dismal down below. So now she watched them casually, or what she hoped appeared that way, because her curiosity was up and this was the safest venue to learn more.

The lady looked tense, holding her arms tight against her sides, her shoulders tight and her face disgusted. The other man, the one formally dressed with a ruffled shirt, fancy cut frock coat, britches and high-top boot, tried to console the woman and talk to Lord Leader, she decided to call him. But the man himself looked distracted, as if he was searching for something and yet not. His relaxed impatience made her want to start a discussion with him but she didn't.

One thing was for sure about that lord, the way his clothes fit, he was like a clothed Greek god Apollo, and he moved with confidence, as if he owned the deck. Masculine and graceful movements, like a mountain lion scaling the terrain.

"Ahem."

She broke her stare and felt embarrassment heat her cheeks. "Yes, sir?"

"Ya seem rather fond of that nabob." He nodded in the direction of the lord she'd just been inwardly drooling over.

She snorted. "Fond of? Rather more along the lines it'll be better to get them off this ship, that's more what I was thinking."

"Right…" He paused and gave her a questioning glance. "And what of your arrival here? Leavin' us ta fly with them?" He pointed to the large war ships that slowly came into view. Even she could see the British flags that flew on them.

A chill ran down her spine. "Tell me he won't jeopardize the ship, all of us, to sail into port just to ransom these three."

The Irishman raised his eyebrows and shrugged. "One would believe not. Ya know him the best, lady. What has he whispered in yer ears?"

She squirmed. That was a personal question and made her wonder if he knew she and Trent hadn't been intimate over the last four days. The last time set her head to hurt. It was like she knew the lord but how or where she couldn't place. In fact, he caused her head to pound whenever she tried to figure it out and when nothing solved her issue, she frankly avoided the dreams that didn't wake just yet.

"He's whispered nothing," she admitted. "Spends his time looking at those manifests and checking charts and maps." She sighed. "I don't understand. Whatever is in there makes him edgy." Or he was mad at her. The last time they made love, a tear escaped her eye and she actually fought to keep others back. For as much as she enjoyed being in his arms, feeling him deep in her, it now didn't feel right. It was the why that escaped her, or that she was avoiding.

What she didn't realize while her mind contemplated what was happening to her, Fitzgibbons knelt and tipped her chin up with his fingers. She shut her eyes but knew she had to open them and when she did, she saw a sad smile on his lips as his fingers wiped away a tear. Her blurred vision, her eyes brimming with tears, made her angry, for she couldn't understand why they came now.

"Och, dear girl," he spoke softly, a gentle smile on the pirate's lips. "He's discovered the clue he's been aching fer, if'n you'll pardon me," he nodded.

Outside desire for her, his only other need was vengeance for his wife's death. "For his vengeance?"

"Aye." He smiled. "Thinkin' if'n he's correct, than all shall be good. And you, a place fer home."

She frowned. "I will not leave his side."

"Aye, lassie. He knows." But the tone of his voice made her heart fall into her stomach.

She had refused to return to England and into the hands of whoever abused her. Whoever the villain was, he had taken her memory and replaced it with fear and dread. No, she'd refuse again. She wanted to scream as the pain returned to her head.

"He'll not let you hang, like us, if caught."

She rubbed her arm. "I've heard that mentioned a time or two." She shrugged and tried to smile. But Fitzgibbons' expression was cold.

"You," he started sternly. "The capt'n is right. Yer too much a lady ta stay wit a group like us."

A lump formed in her throat. She blinked and tried to swallow it but it wouldn't clear.

"Rest, lady." Fitzgibbons touched her arm, grabbing her attention back and with a nod, he walked away.

Elle stood on the deck, alone. Feeling for the first time since arriving that she was just dismissed. She didn't like it, not one bit. Her toes curled on the deck as thoughts raced through her mind. So they'd keep her from turning pirate, to keep her from hanging... Trent had issued those very words to her. She bit her bottom lip, irritated, surprised, and annoyed.

Rolling over Fitzgibbons words, she wandered the deck. Stemming the tide that threatened to spill from her eyes kept her occupied. She came to a screeching halt as she ran into a wall — a wall made of flesh and muscle.

With a gasp, she stumbled back but the wall became man who grasped her arms to steady her. Her eyes widened for the one that held her so tight was none other than the nob.

What was his name?

Chapter Twenty-Two

HE WAS BEYOND AGGRAVATED. IT was really a combination of hunger, decent sleep, a bath, fresh clothes, and, oh yes, freedom that really got him going. Three days in that cell. Three. With only minimal amount of time to stretch and inhale sweet air on the deck, a luxury that only he could persuade the pirates they were good for. Especially if they expected money in return for their lives, for James doubted they'd be worth a damn if they were emaciated and on the verge of death, sitting in their own filth…a truly disgusting thought, but it was there.

The bright sun reflecting off the ocean made him squint his eyes as he straightened, stretching. Clearwater and Lydia hovered together off to the side. His patience was about through and they didn't help the matter at all. The past three nights had Lydia halfway sobbing in her sleep, the rest of the time in a foul mood, constantly complaining and telling James she was ruined. Clearwater held better decorum but that was mostly because he didn't weep.

James was bitter also and as time past, he turned inward, as if he sat in a school house, expecting the instructor to beat him. One thing James had noticed was the fact the pirates did not carry any weapon, except for the man who occasionally watched over them in the hold. What he did catch was the men who gazed upon Lydia, leaving no doubt of their desires. So now he had her to protect as well.

Inhaling the ocean breeze, he ran his fingers through his hair, wanting to meet this pirate captain. Eleanor was his wife and by all rights of the British Empire, he would get her back. If she wanted to come back. He squashed that idea. She was his and even Lydia knew that.

He closed his eyes and let the roll of the salt water surrounding them drown out the other noise, mostly in his head. The sun beat down on him, giving him strength he didn't know he missed. The time had come to discuss the issue with this pirate—Eleanor was his. Period. Not a plaything for that thief. The mere thought of that man touching her brought his anger out in full force. One emotion he needed to curtail if he was to be rational enough to win.

Suddenly, someone bumped into him, nearly knocking him off his feet. He silently cursed as he grabbed hold of the person's arms, just to keep himself from falling. He shouldn't close his eyes, knew better actually but exhaustion threatened and he was short-tempered anyway over Eleanor and his compatriots with their constant conniving and complaining.

James did a double take—Eleanor. He was afraid to blink, that she might disappear. In the days he'd been imprisoned here, he'd only seen her the once, with a glimpse periodically, like a ghost for she disappeared that fast. Considering the space on the ship was small, too small to keep them apart, he was thrilled.

She stared at him, open-eyed and wary. One full minute passed in silence before she hissed. "Let me go. You are hurting me."

Surprised by her words and tone, he instantly released her. "Pardon, my lady. I did not mean to stand in your path." He realized his tone was harsh but he was at a loss so more formal was better.

She pulled herself up, as if steeling against him as a man. Her jaw tightened. "I beg apologies. I did not look to where I was headed."

He blinked. "No apologies needed. I stood here, dreaming a dream of what can never be." A dream of her, back in his arms...

A flicker in her eyes caught him off guard. This woman was his wife, the love of his life. But something wasn't the same, outside of her unusual garb, definitely not attire for Almack's or any other ton gatherings. She peered at him now, as if they'd never met.

"Do I know you, my lord?"

The innocent question sliced through him like a rapier—very fine, very sharp and the pain cut him in two. Her inquisitive look never wavered and it, her question and the current circumstances made him wonder.

"Let me introduce myself, my lady, and please excuse the lack of manners." Hell, proper etiquette demanded someone who knew them both do the introductions but the reality was, he did know his wife. "Lord James Haddington III, Earl of Windhaven, at your service." He bowed.

Her face lit up with a grand smile and a sparkle in those sparkling blue eyes. A giggle escaped her lips as she tried to school her outlandish response. "An Earl, you do say? How splendid! I knew you were a nabob, but that sounds like a high-ranking title to me!"

That was not the response he had hoped for. "And if I may ask my lady of her proper title, so I may address her correctly."

She frowned. Once more, not what he expected. Slowly, a smile etched across her sun-kissed face. "I'm Elle," she snorted. "Lady of the *Equuleus*. Nice to make your acquaintance." She extended her hand.

He returned her jovial grin as he took the proffered hand and placed his lips to the backside. "The pleasure is mine. Tell me, how does a fine lady, such as yourself, come to mix with such a perilous lot like the brethren here?"

"I'm afraid I just fell in, one might say." Her jovial expression dissipated, replaced by a straight face, like a child that spoke the truth but quickly hid that fact by changing moods. "But the fit is good, so I am one with them."

"Hmmm," he muttered, battling the inner demon that wanted to shake common sense into her, as well as re-stake his claim to her. "'Tis a dangerous life, one with a noose at the end. Would be a tragic end to such a beautiful lady, one whose beauty would have the world beckon at her feet."

Her cheeks reddened as the smile returned but her gaze dropped. "You flatter."

He took her hand. "I speak the truth. Just say the word and watch even the lowliest of sailors bend to your command."

She glanced away, a troubled look on her face, as if she was confused. Absently, she pressed two fingers against her temple, a strained look in place.

"Are you well, my lady?"

"Of course. 'Tis the sun. Noontime is the hottest part of the day. Perhaps you should have stayed below."

He gave her hurt look. "And miss the beauty before me? The chance to pass words without hope? Never."

That made her laugh. "Ah, perhaps." She leaned closer, close enough the very fragrance of her was almost touchable and he so wanted to run his fingers through that. "But the ears on deck are more keen than the few below."

"A fact well known," he replied, darting a glance about him. "Yet, the lack of two I know is welcomed."

"Your friends?"

He nodded.

She turned, finding Clearwater talking to Lydia near the overhang of the deck. They stood close to the shadows which shrouded them from close scrutiny. Made James wonder what they were discussing while tucked away. It didn't matter. He gave Eleanor his full attention.

Eleanor tilted her head. "She's pretty. He appears full of himself."

James openly laughed. "My lady, I believe you may know them after all." When she smiled at him, his stomach clenched. Her beauty still knocked him over, driving his desire and devotion. Even dressed as a pirate, dancing on a pirate's ship...and a jig around a hangman's noose. His drive to save her hardened.

She frowned, her mouth twisted as if she chewed on a thought like an edible object and it didn't taste right. "I don't believe so, nor you..." Her voice faded and he noticed the slight tremble in her. She knew Clearwater and he'd bet she had run into Lydia over the years. The ton was a tight group, always knowing and watchful of those who entered its midst.

He wanted to lighten her desperate look but was at a loss on how, standing on the enemy's deck, under scrutiny by the pirates but his own people, too. So he did the only thing he could muster so fast—a warm smile and a wink.

That move had caught her attention a year ago, at the Swathington's ball…

She must have remembered it for she laughed, the worried look vanished. "Apologies. So much is clouding my thoughts. Please pardon me." And with that, she slipped out of his grasp and around the capstan, ducking out of sight.

"*Damn!*"

"My lord."

Startled, he glanced to the left and found a youth, his voice crackling.

"Capt'n Cav'ndish be seein' ya now." The barefoot boy turned to lead the way.

Lack of manners or not, James would follow and learn more about his wife and the man who seemed to possess her.

TRENT STOOD ON THE UPPER deck, feet firmly planted behind the table that held maps, journals, telescope, sextant and a sword. He faced the ocean, surveying the waterway and land in the distance that very slowly grew closer. But his recent focus was the scene below him, of Elle and that captive nobleman. He wanted nothing more for her than to rediscover who she truly was, and he believed that she held a status with the ton.

He snorted. He was well aware of what the ton was. At one point in his life, he had been a vital part of that group…what was once a lifetime ago, when he was young and in love. Memories crashed in and sent a flutter to his stomach, one that he instantly fought to contain and smother. Those days were history, a world centered around money and titles and Rachel. If he could reverse the sun and moon to return there, he'd do so much different.

The clip of boots on the deck below, followed by the snaffle of leather on the stairs returned him to now and the nob from below. The one who had been way too close to Elle. His hands clenched as the roll of anger flowed through him now. She was his, not some worthless noble-man…though, and inner voice whispered, maybe he was the one. His fingers snapped the writing instrument in half, right as the man's head raised above the decking.

"Lord Windhaven, welcome." Though he halfway didn't mean it. What did irritated him was he'd bet his ship that the man knew something, was something, to Elle…

The man stood like a man used to being in charge and that this situation was insulting. Trent agreed but didn't care. It was a means to an end.

"Are you finished with us? Release us to the island?"

Trent leaned back, eyeing the man carefully. He was furious but somehow Trent would bet it was on more than being held prisoner. "Close. All this affair on exchanges does take more time than desired." He sighed, more for dramatic effect than necessity and stared at the man closely. "To another matter, your fellow travelers, what names do they hail to?"

The man's mouth tightened. "Lord Clearwater and Lady St. Martin."

Trent's brows climbed as a thrill raced through him. "Viscount Clearwater?" The name clicked in his head and the source hit with a force when his eyes focused on the bound manifests that were on the table. He frowned. "Tell me what you heard of Clearwater Shipping."

One of Windhaven's eyebrow inched up. "It is not something I delve into—trade, that is, not to specifics."

Trent chuckled. "Not worth your time?"

"Not something I have much interest in, outside a few

investments." He stood silent for a moment before he added, "As to this company, 'tis their ship we sailed on, as you are well aware."

"And Lord Clearwater's interest?"

"Going into legitimate trade now?" Windhaven bantered.

Trent didn't answer. Both men watched the other, as if challenging the other to break. Trent admitted to himself he wanted more out the man but nothing came. In fact, the nobleman stared over the ocean, silence filling the air. If nothing else, that intrigued Trent further. What did a lord care over business of trade? He was sure the young titled lord below cared for little more than the next soiree, drink, and loose woman. So why did this one falter?

"I have interest in that company, yes," Trent answered. "Especially its eastern trade."

He paused, noticing the man didn't move. But memories of him talking to Elle returned to his mind. Windhaven was polite but also something more. Did he know her? And did Trent truly want to know, only to feel the need to release her with them, so she could return to her life? He waggled his lips as he tossed and turned the idea.

"Have you ever been in love, sir?" he queried. Images of Rachel mixed with Elle tugged at his thoughts.

Windhaven turned, a guarded look on his face. "What has that have to do with our release? Or trade?"

"More than one may think."

The nobleman was quiet for a moment. "I am."

Trent bit back a smile, because he didn't doubt it, but who? If it was Elle, wouldn't he proclaim so?

"And where is this English flower?" he asked, curiously.

The nobleman glanced away before he answered. "That is not your concern," he snapped.

So, she wasn't involved closely with him. Pity, for the

man could truly take good care of her… Another voice, deep inside Trent, argued he could as too, when all was said and done. No, Rachel's revenge was so close, he could taste it.

"True, to be with you now would be dangerous. Placed on a pirate's boat, involved in intrigue is too harsh for ladies."

Windhaven snorted. "Lady Windhaven is a strong, resourceful woman." He halfway smiled, as if lost in memories. "She's beautiful, graceful, and of good mind, handling everything with ease."

"Yes, but she's still a member of the fairer sex," Trent murmured, his own thoughts on Elle. "They sometimes put themselves in situations that are less desirable and require a man to save them from."

"True." The word was flat, but with a flair of iron to it. It made Trent raise his brows in question. The tone intrigued and irritated him.

"Do you have some issue, my lord, that we need to address?" Once the question left his lips, Trent wondered what pushed him to ask. A quick glance beyond showed him the coastline was changing as the *Equuleus* past the outskirts of British control, though not beyond their reach, and past Port Charles, en route to the Clearwater port. His goal moved closer. He bit back his smile.

JAMES STEAMED. THIS POMPOUS ASS spewed about love and trade while the men around him cursed like pirates and readied guns for a fight, here, in Jamaica. Frankly, James didn't give a damn about any of this. All he wanted was his wife back and for them to be free. But he schooled his anger and waiting for the opening Cavendish just presented.

"Yes, I have requests. You spouted of love and all that entangles, including the fragile nature the fairer sex possessed, yet you keep a lady here. From her appearance, it could be easy to confuse her as your courtesan or a whore." He gritted his teeth on this statement, for he'd seen Eleanor and while he realized something was wrong, everything seemed right. The mere thought that this vermin touching her made his blood boil.

The pirate's jaw tightened, anger evident in his eyes. "Yes, of course that is how you would view the situation."

"Why is she here? And how dare you push her to participate in your illegal pursuits!"

Cavendish said nothing but never broke his locked gaze with him. If it weren't for the pirates aboard, James would attack the pirate captain here and now.

Instead, Cavendish leaned back with a look of total control. "She joined us of her own accord. There is no forcing that woman. Whatever her past is, I do not know nor do I care. Your other accusation is unfounded and ruins her reputation when you have no means to do so, nor will I allow it."

James clenched his fists. "I have every right. That lady is Lady Windhaven, my wife!"

A look of surprise flashed across his face. "That's a rather wild accusation, considering."

"Hardly. She was attacked two months ago, help captive for money but broke free. Whereabouts unknown, till now." He leaned forward, fists on tabletop. "And now, you've placed her in a place of dangerous position—she'll hang, as a pirate, because of you," he seethed.

The captain flinched. It was a very subtle gesture but James saw it. But then, he gave a hint of a smile.

"It appears, lord, that we are in love with two different women." He motioned for him to leave and a pirate appeared, from where James didn't know, to escort him. James sidestepped out of the way.

"She is my wife. I will take her!" It was his right. Clearwater was correct on this.

Cavendish snorted. "I am captain. My word is law! If I chose to divorce you, I will and it will be law."

James's first inclination was to belt the man, mid-section, hard and good. Fury raced through him that this vermin would even consider making such noise but in the back of his head, the tiny bit of rationality, the small portion of his mind, finally spoke audible words. He could make the decree and it had the slightest bit of possibility to be hold truth. Damn!

"You lie. You would have a difficult time reinforcing that. By English law, I am right."

Cavendish's flickered with conflict before he resumed his smile. "But we are not in English territory." Yet... "We are at sea, where I am king." James matched him in height and the two stood, face to face and he felt the anger raging off the captain equal to his own.

Cavendish stared into James's eyes but James wouldn't back down. Damn the man! And whatever spell he had on Eleanor! The mere thought of that thief's hands on her nearly drove him to madness.

"Yet I do hold the proper hand. She is mine."

Cavendish smiled. "Why don't we let the lady decide?"

His blood surging, every aspect of him wanting to rip the man apart, knew the feeling was reciprocated and in that respect, James found himself recognizing Cavendish as an equal in the world of profit and survival despite despising him. Still in disbelief at that realization, James nodded. And the attitude reflected in the man before him equaled his—the competition was on.

Rules were set. He needed Eleanor to recognize him or

he'd have to woo her all over again, to save her life.

Chapter Twenty-Three

ELLE STOMPED DOWN THE STAIRS, furious at Trent for refusing to listen to her pleas about the captive. Though as she lowered down to the hull, she quickly learned storming off barefooted was dangerous as she stubbed her toe on the ladder. She winced but other than that minor peep, she managed to keep the yell inside her.

Her main reason for going below was to take another peek at the captives. Something drove her, what she couldn't name. Perhaps it was what Windhaven mentioned, that she did know them. Gritting her teeth, she continued toward the cell, her curiosity growing.

Only two of the gentry were inside the barred cell. The fancy-clothed man was curled on the cot, eyes closed. Her first impression was he was pretty, all white and pasty-skinned, dressed to the hilt in elaborate clothes, ones that made her garb look shabby and poor. The woman was beautiful, even after being thrown into the hold, in a dank cell, for three days. Her dark brown hair, almost black in color, remained piled on top of her head, a few stray tendrils loose on the one side, touching the nape of her neck.

The demure lady sat on the stool as if posing for a por-trait. The way the sunray, that highlighted the cell, making her appear as if blessed by the orbs, showed her ivory skin, her high cheekbones, her slender neck and the dip of her bodice. She looked up and her gaze locked onto her, even though she thought the shade hid her. Her dark brown eyes sparkled and her coral lips curled slightly, as if beck-oning Elle closer.

"A lady pirate," the goddess spoke. Even her voice flowed like satin. "Tell me what it's like?"

Elle was too busy watching and analyzing her to realize she asked her a question. There was something about her that triggered her thoughts racing, trying to figure it out. Suddenly, it hit her the girl spoke. "Pardon me?"

"Piracy. Is it as wild as they say it is? All the men, the sword fighting, the treasure? Did you jump at the chance to go beyond the realm of propriety and live life?" The woman's eyes seemed to burn with jealousy. Made her stop and rethink the last months of her life, or the months she remembered. But nothing came…

"It is…" she paused, trying to find the right words, "dif-ferent from anything I ever knew."

The lady stared at her, the glare almost a burn. It made Elle twitch inside though she fought to not show it. Some-thing about this woman made her stomach twist. Out of the corner of her eye, she looked to see if the dandy on the pad was awake but he didn't move nor open his eyes.

"Have you been involved in the attacks?" She smiled. "Jumped on deck, like you did on our ship? Lift a blade against another person? Maybe even liked it? And what of the spoils? Do you feel justified in taking what isn't yours, in the name of piracy?"

She swallowed. The verbal attack through light-toned questions, made her queasy.

"I have done none of those things." She tilted her chin up a notch. "Though I was trained in the sword—"

The woman laughed. In fact, she giggled enough to start tears. "Pardon moi. I get ahead of ourselves." She struggled to control her emotions. "Perhaps I just started questioning without introductions." She smiled. "I am the Lady of Windhaven, Lydia."

Elle's mouth started to open but she shut it, as the awe struck her. This beautiful creature was married to the man topside who touched a part of her she didn't know existed. She had felt a connection to him, one that made her stomach flip with butterflies, only to find this out. She swallowed hard. Now her gut clenched, as if it had been kicked. She forced a smile on her lips.

"Nice to meet you, Lydia." Her mind raced. Confusion set in. Lydia might know who she was, but if it meant she'd awake to a world of orders, manners, and stabs at others, she'd remain deep at sea. Doubly so if that handsome man, Lord Windhaven, was her husband. Though she'd just met him, in a true sense, she decided, via conversation, she felt a pull towards him. Something that hinted at he knew who she was, too, and in her mind, she danced with what ways that might mean, but now, she needed to get away from them. For this type also triggered alarms inside her mind of heathens running after her…"I mean, Lady Windhaven. If you'll excuse me, I'm needed upstairs." And with that, she turned and fled.

L YDIA WATCHED HER SCAMPER UP the stairs in her haste to get away. Her lips curled in satisfaction.

"That was quite a performance."

She twirled and found Clearwater eyes wide open as he remained on the pallet but propped his head up by his hand. "I simply meant to clear the field, as it were."

He snorted and sat upright. "James will have your head."

She frowned, her hands on her hips. "I believe your plan was to drive her away from him. I simply aided you in that manner."

"Right." He stood and peered through the bars toward the stairs. "Rickety old thing. Amazing it didn't collapse." He turned towards her. "'Twas a falsehood, to tell her of your supposed marriage to him. But what I don't understand is why she didn't call you out on it."

Lydia laughed. Pure enjoyment filled her very soul. At last, James would be hers, despite her current situation. "She has no memories."

"What?"

"Well, while you and James sat bemoaning our predicament, I found out about her condition." She sat on the only stool, total excitement replacing fear she had of telling the lie. She leaned in, lowering her voice. "They found her in the hold in London. She apparently fled some felons who had pursued her through the docks and she jumped onto this ship to hide without knowing if they were leaving port or not. She fell into the hold and hit her head on something, making her lose her memory." She sided up to him and her voice dropped lower.

"With no recollection as to who she is or who she was married to, I took advantage, and gave her a viable solution. And," she smiled at him, "who else to save her but a trusted friend, Albert Summers, the Viscount of Clearwater."

He paused and looked away. She couldn't see why he would be against her statement.

"Here I give you the perfect opportunity to step forward and claim the prize you've sought. As long as you don't destroy this one like the last one…"

"How dare you, Lydia," he snapped. "I allow certain privacies, but here, you exploit them. I did not ruin the last. That was my father's attempt for Lionel. The pirates overstepped their bounds with that one. Her death has nothing to do with this." He ran his fingers through his hair. "*Damn!*"

Lydia sat silently, letting him rage. She knew Clearwater well. They'd spent many an hour discussing what they really wanted and not what they'd been held accountable to have. He wanted Eleanor. Had wanted her prior to James meeting her, but her marriage to his best friend nearly set him on fire. And not that her thoughts hadn't equaled his, for she wanted James just as badly but was saddled with gentry. Wattsmore would be easy to dispose of for James. While divorce was nie impossible, one of nobleman and gentry could be arranged in the shadows.

"Perhaps you are right." He plopped down on the pallet. "Now the message is to convince James she's too spoiled by this pirate to take back?"

"What a pity," she replied in false pretense. "But from what I've heard, would be easy to do."

"How did you come by this information?"

She leaned back and sighed. "You two bickered and I went looking." She smiled.

Now Clearwater gave a real laugh. "I'm not sure who is worse—you or her?"

Lydia leaned forward, knowing her position gave him ample gaze down her neckline. "Oh, I know I'm far worse."

On that, Clearwater relaxed and Lydia grinned. All was working perfectly.

☉☉

ELLE STORMED INTO THE CABIN, her mind still trying to make sense out of the day. These English nobles were irritating! They were gorgeous creatures, compared to the muck that pirates allowed themselves to fall into—Trent being the exception. They wore their righteous attitudes on their sleeve, as if it were armor. Silky tongues and demanding, that's how she'd view them. And that woman managed to destroy her evening, her marriage to the lord who had made her laugh was the worst of it all.

She slammed the door in response to the painful temple.

"Do we have a problem?"

She glanced at the table, focusing through the red that screened her eyes by the haze in her mind. There sat Trent, his nose in those bound manifests taken from the other ship. A cup on the table, next to a bottle of rum, made her think he'd been here a while. She was about to make a comment when she noticed a few sheets of paper before him on the table. One had Divorce written across it in his handwriting that peaked her interest but before she could ask, he spoke.

"Tomorrow, we should make port. I'd like it greatly if you'd avoid the business that'll take place. It is a dangerous affair, one I'd like to keep you from being sullied in."

The stern look on his face made her take a step back. He looked way too serious. It made her frown. She'd rather he'd smile…

"I'll do the best I can. I take it this adventure won't be happening here?"

"No." He sat straighter. "Stay here. No presenting yourself in any way." He downed the rest of his cup. "So tell me, what has you so flustered?"

She swallowed, instantly worried about tomorrow. What if he was hurt? Killed?

"Nothing, truly. Just," she stopped and went to him, "those noblemen. Must we continue to lock them up? Are they really a problem here? There's only three of them."

The look he gave her, one of speculation, made her gulp. How could she explain a feeling of guilt, of responsibility for their welfare when she couldn't figure it out herself? Especially when her own memory eluded her except for the connection to them. She shook off any idea of trying to argue that with him. He was a pirate…

He chuckled. "Then let it be so. I'll let them roam the ship, but under careful watch. Don't need any mischief from them. Since we'll deposit them anyway tomorrow, I see no reason to allow them to stink up the hold any longer."

"Really? Oh, Trent, that'd be wonderful!" She spun to fly out the door when his arm reached out and snaked its way around her, holding her firmly against him.

"Let their feet wander." He bent down and kissed her. "On such good news, let us celebrate."

She threw her arms around his neck and returned his kiss passionately. Unable to pull away from her, he gently picked her up into his arms and carried her to the bunk. She didn't want to think, didn't want to try to figure out from the entangled thoughts and the clues presented by the noblemen, what this all meant and if her past was linked to them. Instead, she'd relish in the arms of the rugged pirate. Passion took control. Clothes were strewn across the cabin along with the bedclothes.

Entwined in bed, they teased each other to the point of explosion. The moans and groans, musk filling the air until they joined. It slowly registered in her mind that their lovemaking was quick, animalistic in a sense. As if possession of the other, particular him of her, was the primary reason for this intercourse. Maybe it was his attempt to take her as his only for in the midst of their erotic play, Lord Windhaven stood at the edge in her mind. As if he belonged there instead of Trent.

That thought struck home right as Trent drove his final thrust in, setting off the million stars that burst in her mind as she shattered beneath him. Or was it the lord?

Chapter Twenty-Four

JAMES COULDN'T SLEEP. SINCE THEY opened the door to the cell and walked away, James waited for the other shoe to fall. They had locked them up for four days to now, within sight of land, let them free on the ship. It was the not knowing why that disturbed him, for he didn't trust the lot of them.

Under the moonlight, he found only the watchman, way up in the perch on the main mast, was up. Others slept. Some down below, some up here. One thing he did notice was their arms in close reach, even as they dreamt. He stared down at the captain's cabin near the back of the main deck. A twisted thought grabbed him, telling him Eleanor was in there, with Cavendish and by the telling of no lights, entwined with him in ways James didn't want to know.

It was then he heard the door to that cabin open. It was a quiet noise, not stirring a mouse. But to him, it registered. He stepped back to the overhang, near the stairs to the upper deck. He wasn't sure if it'd be her or the captain, so he waited.

Dressed in a loose white shirt and dark, britches untied at the knee, Eleanor stepped out, barefooted. She put her fingers to her temple, massaging the area as she looked out over the dark sea. She appeared lonely and lost. Lydia made comment of her visiting briefly and that little interlude, mixed with his own experience, brought one conclusion—on her escape from the vermin in London, she did literally fall into the ship, as Cavendish had claimed, and that fall made her hit her head and lose her memory.

How did he get his wife to remember him under this set of circumstances presented here? It explained her turning to the captain for protection and wearing pirate clothes, but taking to his bed? His fists tightened at that thought. The captain did rule at sea and James feared he could legally end his marriage to her and the pirate seize her for his own. Simply unfathomable!

"Eleanor," he called softly. The captain called her Elle. Perhaps if she heard her proper name, she'd be cured. But she didn't move. "Eleanor."

Her shoulders shook. Puzzled, he went closer. She was in tears.

"Oh, my dear lady, don't cry." He wanted to hug her. It felt like heaven to have her so near to him and he concentrated on that, trying to kill the thought that she probably just came from Cavendish's bed.

She turned and looked at him. Her eyes were heavy with unshed tears and under the moonlight, her sapphire eyes glowed brighter. "You called me Eleanor."

He smiled. "Because that is your name, my lady."

She frowned as she pulled out of his arms. The look of surprise in her eyes quickly turned to shock and even terror, emotions that struck him hard, as if he'd been hit in his gut with a sledgehammer. He expected happiness, a thrill even, not this.

"No, I have no recall of that name."

He took her hand in his, softly rubbing it. "It is your given name. And your full title is the Marchioness of Windhaven."

Her gaze widened. "I had been your wife?"

His wife? As in past tense? "Eleanor—"

"No!" Her face paled, even under the sun-colored tone. The wild look in her eyes worried him. Thankfully she wasn't shrieking but her voice was agitated. "If what you say is true, how long were we married?"

Dumbfounded, he tried to figure the time. To him, everything had come to a stop until he found here. How long was she gone? "Four months."

She blinked. "Four? Grieving me didn't last, did it? Or did you just toss me out for her?"

Now it was his turn for surprise. What the hell was she talking about? "I'm afraid I don't follow."

She took another step back, her fingers covering her lips. "Stay away from me." And she took off, around the corner.

What the hell?

CLEARWATER STRETCHED. HE JUST MADE it to the top of the stairs, inhaling the clean ocean air. It was so fresh compared to the confines of the hold. Nothing could fill the chest with garbage more than mildew, seaweed, and rotting wood. As he stepped out on the deck, he replayed the scene between Eleanor and Lydia. Lydia had one stake in this—James. Clearwater knew her husband. Henry Wattsmore was the latest addition to the gentry. He was an oversized buffoon and outrageously extravagant in monetary goods. She'd never want under him but he was a trader, not noble. And no amount of conniving or money would rank him higher than he stood.

He smiled. Lydia's desires equaled his and they bonded instantly upon meeting earlier in the year. Not that he was married to a loathsome lass, but he wasn't married at all and the pressure from his father to find a mate was building. His brother, the heir to the title, had finally wed after the scandal had subsided. It was a nasty affair, to want for a woman he could never have since she was married to another. The debacle of stealing her had not gone as favored. Pity. She was a lovely girl, now long gone to grass. His father's mastermind a disaster.

Clearwater adjusted his shoulders and the crick in his neck popped. Too long cramped up… His eyes adjusted to the darkness. Under the brightest of stars, he saw her. Eleanor. She was a beauty, even with her long, luscious locks cut off. He admired her looks when it hit him she was crying. He couldn't have that. He stepped forward right at the time she came, not looking, and ran right into him.

"Lady Eleanor," he stated, trying to act surprised. "What is wrong?"

She stiffened and pulled free from his light touch. "Pardon me," she stated, wiping her eyes. Confusion and pain was clear on her face.

"Shh, it's all right." He tilted her head, as if to exam her face. "What has happened? Has that pirate gone too far? Bring me pistols and I'll demand satisfaction."

"Oh, no, no, all is fine with Trent…"

Trent?

"Its just that, that…" She stared at him. "Who exactly are you? Will you turn to be more bad news for me?"

"Oh, darling Eleanor, I have nothing but good news. I promise," he whispered, letting his fingers lightly trace her cheek. "I am Albert Clearwater." He paused, waiting to see if that caught her memory. Nothing he could tell registered. "I am the Viscount of Clearwater." He squeezed her hand. "When we return, we will put all of this behind us. The banns will be read and we will be together."

She shook, as if in shock, one that registered in her eyes. "Marry? You and me? I don't understand."

"Of course, darling. You've been hurt. We will bring it all to a close. He shouldn't have chased you. You did the right thing. I love you and always will." He kissed her temple. "We'll put all of this behind us and plan for our future."

She gasped.

∞

JAMES WAS STILL TRYING TO fathom what it was that had his wife so upset. What had Cavendish said to her? He took a few steps, convinced he'd find her and discover what had upset her. He rounded the capstan and headed to the stairs. The scene made him come to a screeching halt.

Before him was his friend, the man he'd known for an eternity it seemed, holding his wife in his arms and kissing her lips. James's fists clenched.

∞

TRENT WOKE, SUDDENLY AWARE HIS precious treasure was no longer besides him. The bed sheet was cool. She'd been gone for a while. He swung his legs over the side of the bunk and got up. He shook the sleep from his eyes and peered out the window. The sky was a deep pink as the sun began its slow ascent to start the day. He stretch and pulled on his clothes.

Today was the day. The day vengeance was sought. He closed his eyes and his mind beckoned the image of his wife. Soon, my love, soon.

He left the cabin for the foredeck where he found Fitz-gibbons and Elle. He frowned. She was crying and his first mate was talking in soothing tones to her. He went straight to her.

"Elle, what is wrong?"

Upon his words, she leapt into his arms and bit back a sob. She swallowed hard, and wiped her eyes. "I couldn't sleep. My headaches," she gulped, "they had returned."

He growled. Lord Windhaven's presence was no doubt the reason. While he wanted her memory back, he gritted his teeth that she should return to him. "So it drove you to tears?"

She glared at him with haunted eyes. Her face showed how anguished she was. He wanted to comfort her but he had his own inner conflict. Tell her who she was or keep her for himself. Yet was that fair? For today, he planned to make the man who cause his wife's death pay dearly. Could he really taint her more with his blood?

Fitzgibbons' expression was somber. If he knew, he'd kill Trent for ruining her.

The sun rose higher.

Chapter Twenty-Five

JAMES PACED THE LOWER DECK, his own thoughts clouded. What had he said that made Eleanor run? Or was it Cavendish? He wasn't sure but he waited to see her. He'd looked but didn't see her out. Granted, he didn't travel to the rear of the deck. Something about her sharing the cabin with Cavendish unnerved him.

Could he take her back? That question managed to sneak into his head in spite of his efforts . It would be Christian of him to do so…heavens, he could hear half the ton whisper that and nod to him. But the bulk, despite the charitable disposition, would give him sympathy at his plight, for how could he fulfill his lineage with an heir when his wife had turned pirate and worse yet, strayed from her marriage bed? Could he take those knowing looks so often given, and live? But the marriage remained the same, for he loved her. And in that, he found his answer.

Settled, he turned to demand to see her and ran right into Lydia.

"Lydia, what are you doing up so early?"

She smiled and preened. "I was looking for you, my

dearest James."

Her sentiment grinded his nerves. "Why? Nothing has changed. They let us free from the cage and we'll be released today. But that is all."

"Oh James," she cooed, stepping closer, touching his arm. "I know it is hard, what with Eleanor engaged intimately with another and having no recall of you or who she is. Think of it as time to start new." She gave him another one of her stunning smiles, though now, he recognized it as a song of the wicked to lure him into a trap. Yet, how had she heard?

"I don't think you understand—"

"Oh, darling, but I do. Albert told me everything."

Clearwater? What had he heard? James hadn't told him about his conversation.

"Lydia, please." He tried to disengage her arms, which had managed to loop into his, as if they were lovers.

"It is good," she continued. "I'll leave Wattsmore for you." She reached up before he could stop it and kissed his cheek.

"What?" He couldn't believe what he just heard. "Lydia, I am still married—"

"Shh," she whispered. "Considering all, I'm sure the entire ton would agree. You're free, as I am, for Wattsmore is no better than a commoner, bedding the working class." She winked.

James stared, horrified. The worst part of this, she was right mostly. His skin crawled.

FITZGIBBONS HAD SEEN MANY THINGS in his life. Some he wished he never had, mostly not forgettable, and what he saw now rankled up with that. He'd noticed the emotional tension between his captain and

Lord Windhaven. It was obvious the girl cared for them both. The fact was, the lord held meaning to her past. For his captain to not push her to find out, and possibly get her memory to return so she could escape the life of piracy with its terminal outcome if caught, Fitzgibbons couldn't understand.

Then the glimpse of her with that other nob, the fob, rubbed him wrong. No doubt, this man too held some meaning, but not the way he appeared to interpret that. Fitzgibbons shook his head. Then to find that lady, the pretty one who straddled the line of harlot, saunter up to Windhaven like she just did, puzzled him. It was like watching a play but he saw nothing good on this one. He feared Elle would be hurt and that he wouldn't allow. Damn to Cavendish, who was hell bent to spill blood today for his lost wife. He'd hurt Elle, too, in his machinations.

Fitzgibbons roared. Enough!

He rounded the corner and threw the cabin's door wide open, startling the quartermaster out of his seat.

"Kendall! I need ya ta put yer thinkin' back ta the time prior ta joinin' us. Gotta figure out this situ'tion before this ship bursts inta flames!"

∞

SHE SPLASHED WATER ON HER face, trying her best to freshen up, but she feared her eyes were beyond repair, swollen and red. She sighed and ran her fingers through her hair, straightening up and contemplating what she should do. Things were starting to make some sense, but still she wasn't sure of it all.

Her real name was Eleanor. Sounded right but she wanted more. Lord Windhaven struck a cord deep within her, of a man who was part of her life. Her heart tugged but it also hurt because of him. If he was her husband, why had he abandoned her for another? That lady Lydia was far from being a lady, telling her so bluntly the news, as if she got satisfaction from it. And then that other nabob, no, gentleman, Lord Clearwater. His affections were overwhelming.

And then Trent. He seemed too distracted, too caught up in his own revenge plot for his deceased wife. Eleanor had sympathy for him but at the cost of her? Then again, lately, she caught him watching her with guarded eyes. Of course, their passion was equally guarded, to the point of missing in a physical sense. She had blamed herself for that, as her thoughts were haunted by another in her bed, other than him. Had that been Windhaven?

With a deep swallow, she pinched her cheeks—a habit from her past, she gathered, as she knew her cheeks had color from the sun. Shrugging on the black frock coat, she lifted her chin up in deference to the melancholy she had and walked out onto the deck.

Trent was before her, on the upper deck, hands clasped behind his back, fully dressed in his finest frock and feathered black hat, a handsome man she couldn't resist. She wondered if he had had another life once, back in England, and if she might have met him there. Why not, since in the last day, she heard of other similar tales she didn't have memories to.

With deep determination, she walked up to him and touched his arm.

"Good morning."

He smiled. "'Mornin', darling. This is not the day to be here, for your safety's sake." He kissed the top of her head and gently nudged her back.

Eleanor stared at him in disbelief. The one time she needed him, under what was becoming a stranger set of circumstances, he pushed away.

"Aye, Capt'n!" The watch high up on the main mast yelled and pointed.

Trent pulled his scope out to see. All Eleanor could see was the land moving closer.

There was a commotion behind them, coming from below. Eleanor glanced over to find James, Clearwater, and Lydia. They were not a quiet trio. In fact, they appeared to be arguing. She frowned and their quarrel lured her closer.

∞

JAMES WANTED TO SPIT NAILS. "You told her what?!?"

Lydia didn't flinch. "The truth. She has left you, in many ways. She's turned outlaw and no longer faithful to you. Why would she think you still burn a candle for her?"

He had never hit a woman before, but this one needed to be slapped. Instead, his hands clenched into fists and his blood pounded through him as his anger mounted. "So you told her I married you? My dear lady, I believe your husband might have an issue with that!"

She smiled. It was a knowing grin, like a Cheshire cat. "He is not a nobleman but a tradesmen. Under the right circumstances, a marriage that can be annulled."

James growled and turned on Clearwater. "And what was that interlude I caught you in last night? Embracing my wife, as if she was not taken."

Clearwater eyebrows raised in a questioning tone. "Lydia is correct. Its been over three months since she was taken, vanished into thin air, only to be found by happenstance in bed with another man, an outlaw no less. By the courts, perfect grounds for a marriage voided."

Had he just heard him right? This man was his friend, but now, he moved on Eleanor?

"You two can go to hell! She is my wife!"

A loud gasp echoed behind him. He spun to find Eleanor, dressed in her fine pirate clothes, standing there, her face paling. She stumbled.

"Eleanor!" James leapt to catch her, as she collapsed into his arms.

"My darling," Clearwater murmured, instantly at her side. James wanted to rip his friend to pieces.

"What in all that's holy…"

Another intruder—the pirate captain and his first mate lagging behind him. Only decent thing was the man pushed Clearwater aside.

Lydia stood off to the side, a look of disgust on her face. "She fainted from the truth of her demise, that's what happened."

Only the Irishman seemed to be practical as he got closer. "Give the lass room. Hard ta catch a breath wit y'all stealin' th' air 'bout her." He finagled her away and pulled out a flask, ripped the cork out with his teeth, spitting it to the side, and tipped her up. "Take a swig, Elle."

She did and promptly gagged as the burning liquor seeped down her throat. Another moment, she coughed a few times but the color returned to her cheeks.

"Thank you, Mr. Fitzgibbons," she said softly, giving him a weak smile. It was a warm look that vanished when she turned back to the four of them, replaced by cold anger. "For the last few weeks, months perhaps, I have been lost." Relying on the first mate's arm, she stood. "I've been haunted by thoughts of ghosts, evil ones who chased me, apparently enough to force me to run and I ended up here, with no memory and no name to recall with the only links to who I was in vague images, plagued with headaches. These men," she made a sweeping motion around the ship, "took me in, gave me food, and clothes, and a place to heal. And Captain Cavendish kept me safe, protected me for all this time, like a gentleman! Only to have you come aboard and throw me off balance, trying to convince me of who I am by telling me lies!"

She turned and looked at them. "All of you! And to what purpose?"

∞

TRENT STOOD DUMBFOUNDED, HATING THE fact his lady, the woman who had wheedled her way into his heart, now accused him along with the rest of betraying her.

He had kept his mind focused. He was so close to his goal, he could taste blood but he heard Elle scream and plans of revenge crumbled. And what he saw only irritated him for she was in the company of those pesky noblemen and had fainted, no doubt due to Windhaven feeding her lies to win her over. That was it, enough! He leapt over the railing to the lower deck, Fitzgibbons behind him.

Now, revived by his first mate—a smart move, but one he'd have to correct, as she was his—he found he'd have to pull out all stops to get her back.

"Elle…"

"Eleanor," she stated. Apparently, her memory was returning, though he doubted it was back fully as she stood apart from her husband.

"Eleanor," he restarted as he took her hand and pulled her closer. "Have no worries. What was is no longer…"

"Capt'n! Land!"

It had been what he'd been waiting for. Trent was ready for vengeance. It was all to end now. But instead, he concentrated on her. Though Fitzgibbons looked agitated. Trent shook him off and returned to Eleanor.

"Lord Windhaven has argued he is your husband, but

without explaining why you ran from him, therefore, for your peace of mind and safety, I, Trent Cavendish, Captain of the *Equuleus*, dissolve your marriage, real or fictional, by decree of being captain."

"What!" James yelled.

Clearwater argued for it, Lydia voiced something he couldn't discern. But it was Eleanor's look of pure confusion that stunned him. Why wasn't she happy he solved her problem?

Quietly, she whispered, "Why did you do that?"

Looking deep into her eyes, he replied, "Because I love you."

"Wait!" James bellowed. "Eleanor, please."

"Capt'n! The men!" Fitzgibbons interjected. The sight of land and potential riches stirred the crew but Trent wasn't leaving this.

"You have no authority to dissolve my marriage!" James argued, jumping to her side. "Please, my love, hear me."

The moment she tore her gaze from his for Windhaven's, Trent wanted to roar to the heavens not again! He could not think about losing another.

Chapter Twenty-Six

ELEANOR'S THOUGHTS TUMBLED. HER TEM-PLES throbbed and her heart raced as the closed doors to her past slowly parted.

"James," she whispered.

Instantly, she saw in his eyes the wonder and sparkle that she remembered his name. "Yes, love, yes! 'Tis I!"

Suddenly, she sidestepped when a force from within hit her hard in her skull. Dizziness threatened and she felt the arms of James and Trent supporting her. It was their strength she needed as her past rushed in and her position rang loud. She was Lady Windhaven, or had been, and a pirate.

She spun, out of Trent's hold and facing James. "So I was abducted and in that short time, you felt fit to take this," she pointed to the snake called Lydia. "As wife?"

His jaw tightened. "No. Lady Wattsmore is currently married to another man."

That wasn't convincing. "But for other than him, you'd have taken her."

"No."

"Yes," Lydia interjected at the same time he said no.

He shot the snake a despicable look, which didn't appear to change her appearance.

"Eleanor," he pleaded. He took a step closer. "I've remained true to you, spending every waking moment to find you."

"Eleanor, darling," Clearwater interjected, drawing all to turn to him. "It is time to leave all this behind you and start new."

James glared. "What the hades are you doing?"

Trent slammed his looking glass closed and shoved it in his pocket. "She is not a particle to be torn apart so all parties get her!"

Lydia stared, arms akimbo but she still wore a smile. "This does not matter to you."

The pirate captain laughed. "That, my dear, is all wrong. This is my ship and I am the law."

The deck broke into a cacophony of voices of the nobles arguing. Eleanor's ears rang, unable to hear them for the pounding of her heart.

"Capt'n!"

"Mr. Bowers!" Trent called back, never taking his eyes off the crowd.

"Coast in range!"

They all turned to see. Eleanor could see the coastline clear. Scattered homes sat on the land with a large mansion just overlooking the coast. She tilted her head, admiring its beauty. It reminded her of life she should know, so different from sitting on a ship, rolling with the seas, on constant watch for treasure.

Behind her, an audible moan, stifled but there, sounded.

"Recognize it?" Trent prodded.

"Isn't that Clearwater Cove?" James answered. "Your father's plantation, Albert?"

The nabob sputtered. "Why are we here?"

Trent's lips curved. The look on his face was one of satisfaction and glee, but with a twist. A shiver shot down Eleanor's back. "I believe your father has to answer to a death."

∞

JAMES DID A DOUBLE TAKE, and shook his head to hopefully clear his ears. Death? Whose death? His mind searched but found nothing the Earl might have done. Eleanor looked puzzled though Lydia was stoic. But Clearwater was another matter. He was as pale as a sheet and his upper lip trembled. Whatever was going on?

"Whose death?" He pushed.

Trent's gaze was of steel. "Rachel Cavendish, my wife."

Eleanor stared at him, open-mouthed.

Shocked, James' brows furrowed. "How? To name a member of the nobility when you sail as a pirate, your wife in tow, why would one waste the time? You are criminals."

"She was stolen from me off a merchantman she was a passenger on. I pursued as quickly as I could. Offered the world but their ship escaped." Trent spat. "Later, I was sent word she died in transport by the Barbary pirates."

James stood, trying to follow the narrative when Eleanor interrupted. "And how would a nobleman team up with pirates?"

"Capt'n Cavendish weren't wit the account," Fitzgibbons offered.

James watched. Trent's expression didn't even flicker. His stance was rigid, feet solidly planted on the decking. "Let us send a greeting, shall we?" he announced to no one in particular. Within a minute, the pirates on deck jumped into action, swerving the ship's guns toward the port. "On my mark…"

"No! Wait!"

James with the rest spun to Clearwater. The man still shaken as before. Why?

"A plea for your father will fall on deaf ears, Clearwater."

Trent's non-use of title made James think hard. Titles, including that of captain, were needed to make society move in their place. Including pirates. But the loss had another meaning, he was sure.

"Ready guns!"

"No! You are making a mistake! He did not kill her!"

That plea made everyone turn to face him, except Lydia.

"Explain yourself." Trent looked furious. If it was his goal to pummel the plantation to the ground, Clearwater' interruption had better be good.

"It was all for love," Clearwater began. "My brother, Lionel, he was in love with her. He was sure she'd annul the marriage if she knew he loved her. You had no children." He shrugged.

"And this brother often falls for married women? Abducts them for personal pleasure?" Trent's voice was tense, angry, and sharp.

"No, no he didn't. But he knew Miss Rachel. He had taken her for carriage rides and such before she married you. He was not in town at the nuptials to stop them. So he devised another plan."

James frowned. "And he knew of the Barbary pirates in order to have her taken?"

Clearwater glanced down. "Not exactly. He enticed our father, who, due to trade goods between here and England, have discussions with them."

"Discussions?" This time, it was Eleanor who chimed in.

Clearwater brought his head up and gave her a weak smile. "Yes. One does what one must to protect interests."

"In other words, he bribes them to leave his cargo alone." James shook his head. This was making the Earl closer and closer to trade.

"Yes." Clearwater straightened, his confidence slowly reappearing. "But plans fell apart and they took her away, to escape."

"They were being chased by me!" Trent interjected. "And they killed her!"

"That wasn't the plan," Clearwater pushed. "But, we did hear of it. Edgar was devastated."

"He was devastated? And what of her husband?" Trent roared.

"Edgar was convinced she'd seek annulment when she heard of his true love." Clearwater repeated, shrugging. "We'll never know, will we?"

On that, Trent bellowed vengeance. "You son of a bitch!" He slammed his fist into the man's cheek. Clearwater fell backward and instantly scrambled to stand before another blow came.

"Captain!" James rushed to pull him off his friend.

"Trent, please!" Eleanor pleaded from the side.

Fitzgibbons jumped in, trying to pry Trent off the nobleman. Yanked out of the fray, Clearwater stood, straightening his frock coat and taking the handkerchief from Lydia to dab his swollen, bleeding lip.

"Abduction alone is a crime but to have her in the hands of those barbarians equals slavery and death!" Trent spat blood from his own cut mouth, the result of the nob actually getting a swing in.

Lydia sauntered up and laced her arm through James's. "Truly, it is a marvel how these events can turn."

James gave her a frown while disengaging her hold. "You talk as if this was nothing more than a fight over dinner arrangements."

"This happened before we knew him," she said, pointing at the pirate. "Why should we care now? He is a criminal by the courts and Albert is not, for he did not participate or plan this, and as a member of the nobility, is protected." She worked her arm back through. "It will be a story we tell to our children."

"What?" That indication meant his children, from her? Not in hell! "I strongly doubt my offspring will mix with yours." He pulled away and took a couple steps to get out of her reach and place himself closer to Eleanor.

His wife wore a confused look on her face. Her fingers were at her temple, applying pressure while her eyes darted about the crowd. He needed her to remember. There were moments, seconds really, he swore she gave the appearance of understanding but was that true?

"There will be none of your heirs from Elle's belly," Trent seethed, wiping his mouth again. He took her arm and pulled her closer to him. She stumbled but caught her footing.

"Trent, please," she murmured, her fingers pressed against her temple. "The headaches…"

"Will pass," he replied softly.

James would have none of this. "Get your hands off my wife."

Eleanor stared at him hard. "Wife?"

Trent laughed. Oddly enough, Lydia joined him.

"She is no longer bound to you. I have freed her, as Captain of the *Equuleus*."

"I swear, you can not break English matrimonial law!" James's nerves were on fire. He went to retrieve her.

"James, if he declared it, here on the sea on his ship, he is right."

James turned to Clearwater. "Now you're siding with the man?"

"Not really," he replied. "Just it is the rule of the seas." He shrugged. "I learned a thing or two over the years."

Eleanor's mouth was open, her lips parted at his declaration. "Wife?"

"No, darling, you are not now." Trent's arms encircled her waist, drawing her to him. He kissed the top of her head. "So you can stay here, with me."

∞

ELEANOR'S HEAD HURT TO THE point she wanted to scream. Images blurred through her mind, similar to ones that haunted before, but now they took shape into people she recognized, like James and Clearwater. That cow, Lydia, was still vague… But words they all said struck home, especially wife. Memories of a ceremony loomed before her. It had to be her wedding. She looked at James. The man was handsome, very gentlemanly with proper manners, no swearing like the pirates, and convinced he was her husband.

Then Trent just dissolved the whole thing. Puff! And she was no longer married. That rubbed her wrong. But when she looked at him, his rugged good looks and determination added to a good man at heart.

"Very good, see darling?" Lydia cooed, swooping in for James. "Now our banns will not be in vain."

"Lydia, stop." James once more disengaged himself from her.

Suddenly, a male hand was on Eleanor's frock sleeve. One that was gentlemanly white and cuffed in lace. Clearwater.

"And now, my lady, I can offer my hand…"

"Albert, what are you doing? That's still my wife!"

Trent exploded, yanking her away from the nobleman. "She is now free to wed me!"

She was on the verge of screaming, all the men vying

for her. A man who was her husband, the captain she'd been involved with, and now another who claimed her. This was just too much.

"Sir, Capt'n," Fitzgibbons called. His tone was low, severe.

"What, Mr. Fitzgibbons?" Trent snarled.

"Well, sir, it bein' that decl'ration you stated. It'd be correct, accor'ing to Mr. Kendall, sir." The Irishman shuffled his step.

"Continue, Mr. Fitzgibbons." Trent sounded angry.

"Sir, 'parently if'n you be deep at sea and remained so, ya might be right. But," the man stopped and pointed at the coast line, "you be British waters. Under their law. So she's still married ta the lord."

"What!"

"'Tis true, sir," Kendall rushed on deck. "I had been trained in law before joining. We are in British waters. You're ruling does not apply."

Trent swore loudly. "Elle, please stay with me. You've seen the adventure and the love. There's more to come." He smiled at her, that devilish grin that stole her heart weeks ago.

"Eleanor, please darling," James called. "I love you. You love me. We've been inseparable until you were abducted…" He paused and glanced at his friend. Silence loomed for a couple of seconds. Was he wondering what she was? James finally spoke. "Are you the one responsible for her disappearance?"

"It wasn't to happen the way it did…"

Eleanor gasped. Memories swept back into her mind, crowding to be heard. She vaguely remembered the two who took her and she shuddered. Hearing them making mention of a nobleman who hired them echoed loud and clear.

"Why?" she whispered. "Why would you do that to me?"

"Oh, please," Lydia started. "He loves you. You were hardly a fortnight as his wife, so what an opportunity to make you see your mistake."

"Mistake? Hardly." James stuck back. He turned to his friend. "So she is the woman you found? The one you loved?"

"Yes," Clearwater snapped. "I've loved her since the moment I laid eyes on her. You don't deserve her!"

"So you stole her, like your brother did Cavendish's wife?" James's tone was of total disbelief. "As we discovered, that didn't work well. Why would you jeopardize Eleanor's life for your mistaken love?"

"It is not mistaken!"

"Gentleman, please," Lydia said, coming next to James. "It all works well. Albert gets his love, I get mine and you," she looked at Trent, "remain untouched."

James whipped toward her. "You were part of this? How dare you, you harlot!"

"It makes perfect sense," she continued. "You will see."

"She isn't soiled!" Clearwater retorted. "Leave Lydia out of this."

Eleanor stood in a maze of memories with this tempest about her. And then it clicked. "You love her," she said to Clearwater, pointing to Lydia.

"No, Eleanor, it's you."

She shook her head. "No, you two have been conniving. I've seen it." She looked at James. "As have you, no doubt." She turned toward Trent. His face was contorted but his gaze upon her was tender. "Darling, you know I must stay with my husband."

He breathed hard. "I love you, Elle."

She gave him a half smile. "You loved your Rachel

more." She stepped closer and touched his cheek. "Please, release us and sail away to freedom. Grieve your wife. I think you've been so bottled up by revenge, you haven't grieved. Our moments were of two fluttering hearts, needy and tender, drawing us together. It was wonderful, but these memories, too, will fade." She leaned forward and whispered. "I will miss you. And the joys of being out the sea with you and Mr. Fitzgibbons and everyone. But I have loved James, enough to marry him. We have a challenge ahead but you've taught me enough about strength that I'm determined to see it through for me and for James." A tear pooled in her eyes as she gave him a tender smile. She knew she'd miss him.

He closed his eyes, bending forward so their foreheads touched. "I will always hold you close."

"Eleanor, my love." It was James, his voice soft and beckoning. "We need to see about leaving this ship."

With a small part of reluctance, she pulled away from Trent. He grabbed her hand and squeezed it hard before she was free of him. A rugged smile came to his lips with a nod of his head.

He was releasing her. As much as she adored him, it was right to go back to her husband. The nobleman waited. He was handsome and the small curve of his lips as she took a step toward him ignited a release of her memories. Scenes flashed back, filling the void of her absence. Wedding, bedroom, dining rooms, horseback riding, and many more. The mere touch of his hand sent a cascade of fireworks off in her mind.

Behind her, Trent spoke with a slight tremble. "She is right. Go. Get your stuff. We will dock shortly. And this one," meaning Clearwater, "will clear this ship and crew, right?

The man nodded. Eleanor noticed that now, Clearwater

and Lydia were tight, standing together, speaking in low whispers.

But Trent wasn't through. She'd seen that look on his face when they had approached prey ships—determination, with anger glowing from his eyes. He planted himself in front of Clearwater, his shoulders locked, neck muscles strained and his hands fisted at his sides.

"Not only will you get us safely into port, you will sign a confession to the death of my wife, a confession you will write, for I will not let you go without doing so."

"If I do that and get you free port, with no patrols, you will release me?" Clearwater's voice shook in a reply that border question and affirmation. He pulled himself up and looked at Trent. "And you won't kill me?"

Eleanor froze. The pirate captain's fists clenched tightly. She could see the veins on his forearm bulging from the tension surging through him. But before he could reply, James stepped into the fray.

"Captain, the Visount is a nobleman. He will do as requested." He shot Clearwater a glance and even Eleanor could see the plea in his eyes for the man to do so.

"Yes, the Earl of Windhaven is right. I will gladly write and sign my part in the awful mess that took the life of your wife." When Trent continued to glare without speaking, Clearwater added softly. "You have my deepest apologies. She was a gem in a world full of power struggles and muck and mire. All I want is to see her smile again. What I did was wrong." He hung his head to emphasize the point.

Lydia stood to the side, silent but her mouth fell open at his admitting guilt.

"You do not have to bow to a pirate!" She seethed. "Your father owns the land here and the port. My father also has strong investments here." She turned her wrath on Trent. "How dare you think you could take on a lord!"

The pirate squinted, his brows furrowed with a look of disbelief.

"Lydia, now is not the time…" Clearwater warned.

"No, it most certainly is the time! He who raids British ships, abducts English noblemen and takes ladies' virtue with no remorse!"

Eleanor pulled back, shocked. The woman knew nothing of her time here.

"You are no better than he," Trent hissed. "You will find life in a bordello will…"

Lydia gasped as the blood drained from her face. She opened up her mouth to retort when James stepped up, raising his hand in the air as a sign of bringing attention to him.

"Whoa, wait here," he started. "Let us re-think this." He got in front of the pirate, as if to shield his friend and the lady, Eleanor thought. She also knew Trent was furious and wanted blood for Rachel's death and her stomach twisted, for she couldn't think of a way blood wasn't going to be spilled.

"Hear me out," James continued. "With signed confession, I will promise to bring this and charges you file to the attention of the magistrate of the island."

Trent snarled. Eleanor knew it wasn't enough.

"I will also implicate his father, Lord Summers, as well. Let the courts settle this. As to Lydia, let us return her to her husband and bring it to his attention his wife as strayed too far from him and needs to be checked on all her comings and goings."

The pirate's gaze narrowed. "I can appreciate your attempt, Lord Windhaven, to save their lives. But I have a crew, demanding loot and will need to appease that or that plantation there," he pointed to the coastline. To

Clearwater's father's holdings. "Will no doubt be in flames within the hour."

James nodded. "Of course. Retribution as not been fully met. On top of the indictments, Clearwater will pay you over twenty-thousand pounds sterling…"

"That's blasphemy!" Clearwater roared.

James cocked his head as he glanced at his fellow noble-man. "Really? Was that not the 'price' set on Eleanor's head, when you thought the situation was under control through those vermin you'd hired to take her?"

Clearwater blanched.

"Uh huh." James turned to Trent. "Will you accept those terms?"

The man snorted and a smile returned. "It is a valiant start."

The tension broke. Lydia started to sob. Clearwater nearly lost his balance but James got to him to prevent his fall. And Eleanor wanted to jump for joy. She raced over to Trent and threw her arms around his neck, hugging him.

"Thank you! Thank you for not taking revenge like you'd planned." She squeezed. "I know that took a lot of control not to give in to it."

He returned the fierceness of her embrace and sighed deeply. "For you, I'd give the world. After vengeance for Rachel," he whispered.

She looked up at him and mouthed thank you when he caught her off guard and swooped her up into his arms and kissed her hard. It was harsh, demanding and so him, she thought, when he abruptly stopped and set her on her feet. The reflection in his eyes was not warm.

"Dear Lord, run back to your husband," he warned. "Because if I'm of a notion to steal you away, with me."

Her eyes widened, surprised after his quick release of

her just minutes ago. In the corner of her eye, she saw James staring at her, a stiff look. He saw the kiss and now waited to see what she'd do. But now, she knew what was right—she spun on her heel and ran to James's arms, the force of her leap to him made him grunt as he gripped her tightly. She squeezed and gave the pirate a glance. His mouth was in a thin line as he gave a short, barely notice-able nod to James before he turned and left them.

∞

"THANK GOD, YOU ARE BACK to me!" James nuzzled her neck. She smiled as it felt right, the feel of him against her. "I love you, Eleanor."

She pressed against him and relished in the return. "And I remember it all now. I love you too, James." She pressed a kiss against his check. But suddenly, she stepped back, a worry taking hold. "Could you ever forgive me for this last month?"

"Forgive you?" He looked puzzled.

She shifted her feet and bit her lower lip. Would he understand that her loss of memory had driven her into Trent's bed?

James squeezed her hands and pulled her up close, tip-ping her chin up so he could look into her tear-laden eyes. "I love you. He saved you and you had no memory. There's nothing to forgive." He kissed her forehead. "All is back to what it should be."

Inwardly, she relaxed. "Take me home?"

"Yes darling." He swooped her up and kissed her mouth, his tongue running the seal of her lips, prying them open.

His tongue invaded and quickly, her own responded with welcome. The kiss was hard, deep, demanding, and beautiful. She sighed. She was home, with the man she loved.

JAMES'S HEART SOARED TO THE heavens when his Eleanor returned to him. The poor organ had taken a sound beating with her abduction and then to find her here, on a pirate ship, in another man's arms. Confusion slammed into him as to why would she run to another when the love they shared was so rich, so deep. That mixed with his desire to kill Cavendish for taking advantage of her out here at sea, a position she found herself in due to an evil side to his friend of old, Clearwater, who she escaped only to fall head first into a pirate's hull and losing her memory. In a sense, he couldn't resist the feeling of satisfaction that the man would have to admit to his crime with the confession and James's own determination to make sure the authorities would have that document. In their hands, Clearwater would pay, hopefully for more than just by the indignation of being under the law.

So he could rest assured, as best he could, that Clearwater would pay yet regardless what the courts said, he'd make sure Eleanor was never in his presence again. As to Lydia, he couldn't help but inwardly revel at the mere thought that she'd be returned to her husband and that man would be informed of her wanton behavior. Despite her beauty, her husband could enforce total reform on her, something that was sorely needed.

But one question remained. Could he forgive Eleanor for accepting another lover?

His heart screamed for her. She was his wife, his life even. He really had no choice but to forgive and take her into his embrace, to show her how much he loved her. From all the arguing around them between Lydia, Clearwater, and the pirate, who glanced at Eleanor one more time but not again, James thanked the heavens for her return to him.

And he'd spend the rest of his life loving her. The impact of that drove into him deep, just like his kiss. *Oh, this love of mine...forever will I love you.*

He wasn't sure if he said the words or if she read them in his movements but either way, her kissing turned ferocious, of the style he understood. Now and forever....

~ The End ~

Acknowledgements

I'd like to thank the Regency Romance Critiquers for being the driving force to get Eleanor and James's story out. To my editor Jennifer Bray-Weber for awesome work! And Jennifer Jakes of Killion Group for helping me in the 11th hour when I lost part of my publishing team! To Kim Killion, who designs the best covers! I also like to thank Cynthia Veldman, Daryl Quellette and Pamala Knight who helped flush out the details that were so badly needed. Thank you!

Other Books by Gina Danna

Her Eternal Rogue

The Wicked Bargain

Love & Vengeance *(The Gladiators, Book I)*

Love & Lies *(The Gladiators, Book II)*

Great & Unfortunate Desires

The Wicked North *(Hearts Touched by Fire, Book 1)*

Author Bio

A USA TODAY BESTSELLING AUTHOR, GINA Danna was born in St. Louis, Missouri, and has spent the better part of her life reading. History has always been her love and she spent numerous hours devouring historical romance stories, always dreaming of writing one of her own. After years of writing historical academic papers to achieve her undergraduate and graduate degrees in History, and then for museum programs and exhibits, she found the time to write her own historical romantic fiction novels.

Now, under the Texas sun and with the supervision of her three dogs, she writes amid a library of research books, with her only true break away is to spend time with her other life long dream - her Arabian horse - with him, her muse can play.

www.ginadanna.com
www.facebook.com/GinaDannaAuthor
www.twitter.com/GinaDanna1